SCARRED VISIONS

Scarred Visions

~ *My Debut* ~

AMAAN SHABIR

Amaan Shabir

Contact The Author

Instagram handle:
@Amaanshabirofficial

Twitter handle:
@Amaanshabiroff

Contents

Scarred Visions
An Anthology About Bipolar Disorder

This material is a combination of dystopian narrative and poetry, all entirely written by the author himself.

First Printing, 2022

Cover images: Istock.com/Wackoma

This book is based on my personal experiences regarding bipolar disorder, from the highs of mania, to the depths of depression and how it has affected me and can affect the rest of the bipolar population.

This is to all those who enjoy my art of writing, and to those yet to discover it.

Thank you to Hunter Keegan for supporting me with this project in the midst of working on it.

Thank you to Scarlet for making this possible. The concept of the euphoric city would not have existed without your help and support while my first drafts were emerging, four years ago.

Visual Cover Production:

Cover Image photography licenced by Istock.com's extended licence: Istock.com/Wacomka

Trigger Warning

Trigger warning:

This book explores topics regarding mania, depression and suicide

Only Read If You Are Comfortable With This

Chapter 1

Mania's Beginings

My blood tastes like dysfunction, and my mind spills blinding colours in a black-and-white world where the extinction of despondency is ever prevailing. A mosaic of falsehood and deception, which I choose to be deceived by, although it's not a choice.

My barren soul once again flourishes with the rivers and oceans of life that feed into my brain, keeping me up for days upon end, and sleep becoming nothing but an unfamiliar acquaintance. Logic and emotion. Which should I choose? It can't be mind over matter, when my mind is the matter.

What the fuck is wrong with me?

Nothing.

I'm purely invincible, yet the smallest thing could destroy and crush my heart and my otherwise indestructible smile permanently plastered on my face. No one who has crossed my path has ever rejected the irresistible urge of knowing my acquaintance or survived the undeniable wrath that I hold with the vindictive side of the power that my mind possesses.

Imagine a place. A place of euphoria. Many people like me are familiar to this place. We love how poisonous it can be, and if I'm completely honest, sometimes a high is worth the price we pay. The price is our health, our relationships, our financial status, and more. We adore how sickly it is. We become addicted and stay there for as long as possible; weeks, months, and sometimes even manage to stay there for years.

But we don't get to choose our stay. The place does. The place is always moving, and sure enough if our lives ever get too boring, we usually will try and do everything we can to make this place arrive with haste. We can be very impatient people.

We've been labelled, stereotyped and branded by society. The truth is we are just sick. Sick of everyone's bullshit, but also truly sick. We have an invisible illness, that claims the lives of many all over the world, and if I told you who we were, you'd call us insane, and that's because you don't understand. So let me take you to this place, and to the other places that we know of.

Chapter 2

AshWays

Travelling There

To many people this place is nothing but a source of fascination to quench a few human minds and provides nourishment to their thoughts. What so many are unaware of is the ever present two sided characteristics that are personalised to each of these places. Each species that manages to call this place home is still learning, through mistakes, the dangers of the place they call home. Adaptations always help but by no means does that mean there are no points of vulnerability. Out there it is each to their own. If they find love then it is by chance, their responsibility to ensure that everyone manages to survive. Survival is the test. Many pass yet even more fail.

Everything acts like minions for the evil master of despondency - he is always trying to catch things unaware. Much like what happens in life; in a constant game of cat and mouse, sometimes the hunter can be the hunted and may feast upon the flowing thoughts of one's own weaknesses. Only very few are immune to this.

To most, it is just a legend: AshWays.

Nothing more than a tale told to those of youthful minds and aspirations- much too naïve and gullible to have known the real meaning of life. There was always a false promise in the light that was once told to us: happiness comes without a price. Then comes the question; to be or not to be? Would one rather settle for the monotonous one life lived by millions, or would he rather sacrifice it all in the unlikely search of what may be just a rose-tinted myth?

So the sun bled her rays into the heavy hanging sky, and sand dunes rolled off into the endless depths of the unknown.

Selfishness is the key to one's saviour. Be kind and you'll be killed. Be foolish and you will win. With many obstacles in his path, one must be wary of the worst: the demons. Evil entities that will devour your thoughts, behaviours and mental states, they are said to be the only source of danger that will manage to crawl their way into AshWays.

A paradox it seems: the euphoric city to be plagued by such creatures, but you can either tame them or let them tame you. No one knows which is the correct fashion. But many know, that as we are not sure of their intentions, they are certain with ours.

A sick sense of humour blessed onto those cursed beings that will corrupt one's journey into AshWays... A constant company that is invisible to the eye, yet everyone can see their affects. One must proceed with caution – the smallest mistake can have the direst consequences. Like a moth drawn to a flame, he continues his pointless journey; in search of a fib that he emphasises is a truth.

His destiny will surely be revealed . To believe or not to believe? That is the question that will have no answer. Is there an AshWays? And if so, how can one access it?

******

A single drop of rain fell onto the golden sand, and I watched as it sizzled and evaporated into nothing- joining the hazy, heavy and unmoving air that swallowed the entire desert wasteland.

Thirst drove my body a few steps forward before I collapsed onto my knees and felt the stinging burn of Earth's merciless wrath. Her blanket of sand tenderly whipped the familiar sensation of pain through my veins as I silently screamed in what people call 'agony'.

My eyes were caressed by the canvas of endless sand dunes that rolled over into the horizon. The entire landscape was a monotonous combination of shades of dusty brown and orange, void of any life or hope. A few metres to my left were the remains of what used to be a dead person's corpse, but now flies, locusts and mosquitoes have inhabited the rotting bones and have made themselves at home to the repulsive aroma of decay.

My body protested as I dragged it a few more yards with all the energy I could muster.

"To get to the AshWays is impossible," they'd said. It's surrounded by thousands of square miles worth of desert, an impenetrable stretch of sand, death and void of all life. No one could enter the AshWays and no one could get out either. The surrounding landscape was extreme, too extreme for even the most avid of explorers to venture into or out of. I had merely crossed the borderline into the desert and was already struggling to keep my bag of bones alive.....

Each passing second extended into what felt like one hundred years , as my swollen lips and tightening throat willed my body to shut down and accept death.

Four days. Four days it has been since I tried getting into AshWays and I have made no progress. Trapped in a sinister playground of misery, my eyes scanned for the slightest hint of a city 'bursting with neon lights', a city that was the 'home of happiness' and broadcasted the rare element of 'euphoria' across its lands and into its citizen's hearts and souls.

It seemed that AshWays was just a fantasy, too good to be true, but people insisted on its existence. I challenged their theories, questioning why they hadn't tried to reach the city themselves.

They responded, ' Those who have tried, never made it alive.'

Now I can see why. In the past four days I must have been blessed with the sight of two-dozen bodies, skeletons and remains of dead explorers. Not the type of explorers who enjoy venturing into new lands- but it's a fact that those bodies belonged to souls who were in search for AshWays, the city that apparently provides its people with what they couldn't find: elation.

They were explorers in search of something that is so rare anywhere else, yet in such abundance in the 'enchanted' city of AshWays. They didn't even make it past the desert. It looked as if I were to face a similar fate.

I was dishonest- my reasons for attempting to travel to AshWays did not stem from my arrogance and doubt, but because I was among those who felt like I lacked emotion. AshWays,; the euphoric city that is beyond reach. There is no point of its existence if no one new can access it.

I don't know how the city is home to people in the first place, but no one has made it inside the city to ask.

The sun collapsed from the sky and swarms of locusts filled what would have been an empty night. The temperature nosedived from searing heat to the cold embrace of night as I cuddled to the floor. No shelter from the locusts, no shelter from the night. No shelter from danger, no shelter from fear. The only comfort I had was the thin brown fabric that clung to me. The fabric that I called, “my clothes.” My eyes drooped and my body fell under the malevolent spell of sleep.

******

One struggles to comprehend the sheer simplicity of the meaning of 'love'. It is the people you meet on accident that make your journey worthwhile, even if it is just a mirage that you stubbornly refuse to 'unsee'. The journey across the threshold is a lonely one. A deep and dangerous venture into the City Of Euphoria: a place ruled by a corrupt government, abandoned yet thriving under the dominance of one's own demons. A place of extremes, inhabited by a mass number of living people who flourish under the City's 'neon lights that burn brighter than the rings of Saturn.'

One must make his way alone: but not alone entirely. His mind will surely be acquainted by several demons, each whispering a secret dirge of hope in a language of behavioural differences. It is one's own 'atmosphere' that creates the first impression, but to many, they have become slaves to the evil entities that whiz around in the playground of his mind.

But he still continues his lonely trek further and deeper through the desert, every step he takes, he wishes to bring him closer to the hope of finding AshWays, but fatigue is a fierce competitor and eventually, he drops his body's weight into the golden sand, the scalding laughter of his demons echo painfully in the centre of his mind. Even though he is a finger's width away from 'death', his mouth curves into a painfully dry and cracked smile. Moments before he thinks his time is up, a canopy of a single shadow blocks the sun's stabbing rays and a living being leans over...

The legend states that there is only one condition to reach AshWays: you must do it on your own.

Yet a brotherly bond has sparked up within the desert. They put themselves in a position of great danger: both have been driven insane by their demons, both are in search for AshWays, both need to be selfish yet both care for each other. Any form of love is vulnerability. Any form of vulnerability leads to certain death. They must abandon each other for their own safety yet their innocence and naivety blindfolds them both. It's a blissful ignorance that will end in an agony of tears and two bodies will lay lonely in the desert sands, as the desert will eliminate anyone who doesn't follow the simple rules the gates of AshWays asks for them. For how can one expect to be welcome into the city if one doesn't make the crossing from the desert whilst following the one simple condition asked of him?

******

AshWays

A Letter

To You,

I bet you thought your journey had ended two years ago, where dead bodies carpeted the haunted streets of what was known as the city of euphoria- AshWays. Let me assure you now, that there is no happy ending to this story. Or to any story. 'Happily, ever after' , the classic fairy-tale ending only lasts until the character finds themselves stuck once again in the labyrinth of troubles, but no one would tell you that.

We live in a world where people would rather believe a sweet lie than the bitter truth. Don't argue with me on this. We both know it's true. The sacrifices you made, the pain that you endured, the tears that you cried and the people that you lost... where has that gotten you? Nowhere. You're still stuck here. Stuck in the same situation, in the same place, with the same pain. You're dumb enough to even think that you'll make it out alive. The calamities you will face will go away, right? Wrong. They'll only return but in a different form. The humans here are a disgusting species. Rotten with hate, division, lust and delusions...; you won't survive. A feeble, weak soul who still clings onto the false hope of love, friendship, and forgiveness- those are exactly the things that will kill you here.

You may wonder why I'm being so hostile this time. It's because you didn't listen. If you remember correctly, I warned you. I warned you about the corrupt society that thrived on the other side of the desert wasteland. The city, abandoned by its own government, but governed by the nature of its own people. I warned you. But advice always falls on deaf ears when the person receiving it is like you.

To survive in the AshWays, you must be hateful. Abusive. Manipulative. Cunning. It's every man and woman for themselves here. Eventually you will die- as will all the residents. When each of us will die is uncertain, but one thing that is certain is that we will die alone.

So, take care of yourself and yourself only. Don't get pulled into the common illusion that everything you feel here is good for you. It will feel that way. But remind yourself of your reality. Time is no longer an acquaintance to me. Once again, I'm having to leave you. Have fun here while it lasts, cos the fun will surely outlive you.

Hope To Talk Soon,
Common Sense.

******

AshWays

Welcome

If you are reading this, then I guess it's already too late. We have been cast aside into the shadows of the city; a place where 'euphoria' presides over the 'sky- scraping' buildings, but the irony is buried six feet up into the atmosphere of this treacherous place.

This wasn't how it always was. This city is a corpse of what it used to be, an echo into the radiant past that it once possessed. Now, all what's left are the bitter remains of a broken urbanised area, free of laws, but full of outlaws.

The annual parade proved to be a homicide; two teenage boys who brought the elements of true happiness in its purest form were slaughtered.

Their bodies and blood create a beautiful mosaic of tragedy in memory of the traumatic events that occurred many years ago. However, the aftermath is still relevant. Wherever you go, the soft crunch of the blackened 'ash' roads will alarm the people of your presence.

The people here are disgusting.

To the North reside inhabitants that are drowned in the obsession of lust and sex, their obscene behaviours are what label their sector of land as the 'root' of fornication and prostitution.

The Eastern sector is home tothe escapers- those in the society who are frowned upon due their constant plea to break out of the city's borders.

The Southern roads belong to the homeless, who are experts in trading illegal goods, which only offer a few moments of mental freedom when burned and smoked. The rest of the intoxicants mix into the sinister atmosphere of an unhealthy air.

The West side of the city is no better. Nestled in the untamed foliage that keeps them captive; the people who reside there are no strangers to the event of a civil battle.

Each sector of the city is personalised with each distinct characteristic. Be careful. Human blood has a dangerous tendency to spill at even the slightest of cuts. Your only bet of getting out of here; is by getting through it; otherwise, you will find yourself imprisoned just like the rest of us. By the time you've read this, they would've already learned of your presence. If I had a choice, I would have sent you off into the desert of golden sandthat surrounds us; and left you to helplessly die of disease, thirst and hunger, which would have been a much more peaceful way to die rather than face the consequences of being here. But I don't have a choice. Make yours.

******

The sight of flickering lights of the tall buildings was what I first noticed as my warm eyestook in the visual attributes of my surroundings. Unmoving air surrounded me; to my skin it felt hot and sticky, carrying the dreadful perfumes of human sweat and blood, whilst possessing a metallic taste of bitter lust and sweet desires.

The roads were bustling with activity as the sun saluted her final farewell and gave way to a blissfully beautiful darkness which contrasted with the bright beacons of colour. A dirge of human chatter filled what would have been a silent night; screeches of laughter mixed with the voices of the inhabitants of this place. There are some here that I love. Some who are frightened of me. Some who want me dead. I didn't ask for this. No one ever does. Being held captive; I am one of them.

Only I'm not.

The disturbing nature of these people is hard to ignore. Feasting on any source of satisfaction they can access; each night is full of the exploitation of bodies, being haplessly thrown into a sinister portal of casual sex. With such an extreme disregard to simple human decency, you would expect that there would be consequences for their actions.

If you did expect that; you've forgotten where we are. We are in the AshWays- and this is how everyone thrives. They find an artificial source of temporary distractions that last moments before being tossed aside and forgotten about. If you're weak- you won't survive.

I'm a survivor. But tomorrow I could lose that title. In a city so unpredictable, anything can happen. It's a paradox. The city is organised in the most frenzied ways imaginable. No laws, no government, and no figure of authority. The people have taken it upon themselves and chosen the lives they wish to live, consequently resulting in their impulsive behaviours.

The city's distinct illumination of neon purple, orange, pink and blue colours birthed from every building, every door, every window, and from the top of every skyscraper. My legs dragged forward as I turned onto a narrow street, away from the main roads. My eyes had been scarred enough already. The stretch of land was relatively dark. I could make out the shape of the cluster of brick buildings that sat despondently on either side of the cobbled street, and instead of the sharp beacons that stabbed the impression of a darkened night, there was the presence of a gentle and welcoming glow that was emitted from each building- not too bright. In fact, they would turn off for a few moments before reviving, reflecting their delicacy.

My eyes focused back onto the sinister street that directed away from the frenzied energies of AshWays's inhabitants. The blood red glow of the flickering lights spilled out from the bottom windows of each building, and progressively dimmed with the correlation of the buildings' height, to the point of which only darkness was present at the top third portions. This street was clearly different. The sky above was a velvety carpet of black, the only stretch of air that was not touched by exotic colours of artificial brightness.

Despite the relative gloom, my pupils could catch every detail of the cluster of edifices defending each side of the street. Fallen pieces of glass presented themselves as a matting of tender pain, along with the dusty presence of sawdust which coated the floor. The occasional gust of wind would toss a handful of the debris into my face, leaving me coughing and spluttering like a child suffering from his first cold.

Markings of white paint seemed as though they had lost the battle to the weathering and were evidently eroding out of vision- indicating no one had considered to resuscitate them. Or maybe no one had noticed. I could only conclude that this individual segment of land had been abandoned and forgotten about, due to its inability to hold masses of people, as its narrow width was its most distinct feature. The poor structures of thedeserted houses, shops and rejected buildings informed me that indeed, not a single soul resided in this area anymore. Their swords of splinters, broken wood and pieces of metal stuck out aggressively, poking their way out of any crack that they could find. And there were plenty. Holes infested each building like a plague of maggots, adding to their breaking beauty.

I saw movement. At first, I thought it was an illusion. But I saw it again. A few metres to the left side of the road, someone was watching me. They were cowering near a rotting door to what used to be a small hostel-, 'Dustpath Hostel' to be exact - those were the words carved into the sign that hung over it. The person was of slim figure and around my height. They wore a black cape and a hood that covered their face. The only skin that was visible was their pallid hands with bright neon blue and turquoise painted nails.

I assumed it was a woman. Having no idea why she was alone, I decided to slowly approach her. The sounds of cracking glass and debris filled the silence between us, until one of us broke it.

"Follow me,." a female voice called out. She didn't wait for a response, dashing into the abandoned hostel, disappearing, and becoming one with the shadows...

AshWays

The Second Letter

To You,

The human mind never fails to astonish me. Such a complex creation, yet sometimes it struggles to comprehend the simplest concepts. It was never the case that your sanity departed, rather you choose to overlook the red flags, or maybe red is just your favourite colour. You are someone who has been blessed with a intellect of huge depth, as you belong to the human race: those who have come so far in the discovery of psychology, psychiatry, and love to ponder about the world around them. Yet you're still too stubborn to look through the logical lenses, and instead follow the emotional hallucinations, which will ultimately lead you to painful consequences. When will you ever learn? In a deadly game of cat and mouse, the hunter can quickly become the hunted. This is a place where many have succeeded yet even more have failed. Tread carefully. Trust no one yet trust every word that they say. They know about this place than you do. Ignorance has never been a bliss here, and never will be, as it has always led to the tragic death of a poor, unfortunate soul. Emotion is everywhere, don't get tangled up in its spiderweb, or else there will be a price that you will struggle to pay....

She has asked for your time and body in exchange for her knowledge, a place to stay for a few nights and her vehicle, which you can clearly drive well when you're not distracted by her physical appearance. But you and I both know appearances can be deceptive. We both know she is a user and abuser just like everyone else here. Don't be stupid. Don't follow your heart. Follow your mind, and follow it into the cunning forests of thoughts, that will sure enough grow in time, the longer you stay here. It starts as a seed, then germinates into a tree, and before you know it, your mind will become a forest of thoughts, ideas and solutions for every problem, calamity and sacrifice you encounter. You will be invincible. But first, you must let the city consume you. It's a deadly cost, I know, and you've probably heard to try your hardest to stay away from the strange folk who live here. Yes, they are users and abusers, but as I said sometimes the hunter can become the hunted. Abuse the abuser. You have the power to. Just time your actions wisely, as sometimes being oblivious does more damage than being aware....

Take what I said and use it as a warning, a threat or a handbook to your survival. Or don't even acknowledge it at all. The choice is yours – it doesn't benefit me either way. We are strangers but you surely know who I am.

But go, follow her, give her what she wants, and take what she has and don't come back. She's stringing you along in hopes of using you and I know that you're aware of it, but sometimes the smart thing to do is to act the fool to fool the fool. Common sense hasn't been a good friend to you, and I'm afraid he's not too helpful either. He doesn't sugar-coat things; he sees the value in truth – the blunt type. I do too – but I hope to portray it in a way that will comfort you and not be as harsh, no matter how high your level of stupidity may become.

I'm guessing he also isn't it a good friend in the context of being there when you need him. That's why everyone uses his name so haplessly. I hope you see me as a more permanent companion, and I'm sure you'll figure out my identity soon. I already know yours – but before I go, I beg to ask, do you even know what you're up against?

Yours Truly,

A Current Stranger.

Chapter 3

Juices

She was playing with dice in a game of cards. Don't underestimate my intelligence, it is sometimes wiser to act the fool, to fool the fool. With the drink in my hand, and myself in the hands of the room's darkness, I lifted the marble cup to my lips and took a sip.

She smirked.

The liquid had a metallic taste that bubbled in my mouth, frothing and increasing in volume the longer I held it in my mouth.

She then took a sip and also held it in her mouth.

I felt my cheeks beginning to expand in protest against the growing quantity of the sparkling juice, but I knew I couldn't swallow. I couldn't let her win. She had fierce eyes of sour green that pierced through the darkness and eerily watched my every move. She had not said much but offered to play this game in exchange for a more fitting disguise to blend in with the residents of the North. She had claimed that I stuck out like a sore thumb, and that anyone who doesn't fit in with the behaviours of AshWays's societies, will be given the capital punishment.

She claimed they would tie up the limbs of any intruders and put them to drown in the surrounding oceans- but this puzzled me. There was no ocean. Only a desert that enveloped the outskirts of the city, but I had let her speak as she knew more about this place than I did, and I was not ignorant enough to let myself question her authority.

"Okay you can swallow now."

I swallowed. The juice fizzed down my throat, bubbles popping against my oesophagus, causing me to splutter in disgust.

The room had a small circular table, at which we were sat, and we both placed our marble cups back onto the wooden surface of the table. She stood up and walked across the room, to open a window, and finally streaks of light dashed into the room, expelling any sign of darkness that once dominated the inside of the hostel. Due to the newly found light, I could finally see the person, the stranger, who I had chosen to trust in this foreign land. She was amazingly easy to look at, and awfully hard to look away from. She had removed her cloak to reveal her slim figure, dressed in blue jeans, and a white blouse which had its first couple of buttons purposely undone. No surprise – It looks like she was also enjoying the promiscuous nature of the people who lived here. Strands of golden silk fell to just beneath her shoulders, complementing her fair complexion, and high cheekbones paired with bright red lips gave her an overall sultry appearance. Under her eyes, were the presence of a few freckles, decorating her already pretty face. Her eyelashes feathered and surrounded her bright pupils, which reminded me of an owl due to the intensity of her stare.

Suddenly, the inside of my stomach felt as if it was being turned inside out, burning and twisting, threatening me to make me collapse. The world became dizzy and spun out of my vision, as I felt myself hit the floor, vomiting out the juices that I had swallowed in a pool of my own acids and the remaining contents of my stomach. She had spat hers out. It was when darkness began creeping into my vision, that I heard her cackle, and heard the sound of footsteps pounding against the floor, becoming more and more distant every second...

Chapter 4

Happiness Is Dangerous

The break of dawn provided light to the Earth's tired surface, as a young character's eyes widened to absorb the beauty of god's creation. With shallow breaths and a pulsating heartbeat, he didn't observe the world for long from his bedroom window; he had his own metaphorical world to tend to; and his brain threw him into a place where the colours of joy were so bright, that it blinded out any valid road of logical reasoning. His eyes followed a pair of birds soaring among the clouds, their bodies becoming nothing but small specks of black against the clementine of a sky. The toxic perfumes of elation wafted up his nostrils and polluted his lungs, replacing the oxygen in his bloodstream and intoxicating every blood cell in his veins and arteries.

A rush in his chest, and pace in his feet, he scampered downstairs, and dashed out the front door, his mind was a portal to awe and wonder. Winter's air bit him mercilessly, her teeth scratching against his delicate skin, but he was numb to any pain inflicted to him. He was bursting with mental energy, and a grin had found itself a home on the centre of his glowing face. The howling wind played her seasonal lyrics of bitterness and despair, but the warmth of his internal body burned an inferno against anything other than immense joy. Eyes dilated, flashing teeth and an impatient body, itching to always move, he ventured through the mattress of white snow that lay itself on the road and pavements, left ruined by the permanent footprints he left behind. He followed the dreadful perfume of spontaneity, held hands with euphoric recklessness and was encouraged by blissful ignorance. Only if he was aware of the danger, he was in...

But logic is not something that can always be present in these lands. He, just like everyone else here, is led by nothing but pure emotion, which will always be heightened for as long as he stays within the perimeters of the North. Trapped, but not trapped, it is a paradox that keeps all the residents from questioning their impulsive actions and behaviours. They see nothing but the bright colours of emotion that brim from their minds and spill into their pupils, blinding them from any danger or consequences that they will surely face eventually. It is a habit of those who live here, to try and escape into the sectors of AshWays, once they realise how delusional and recklessly, they begin to behave while under the influence of the North's air, but travellers never make it far. They might make it through to the next sector, but each sector can be set to kill the people who don't belong there. Our protagonist belongs nowhere. He is an intruder to all parts of the city- someone who came from outside and forced himself in. He must keep a low-profile, or else he could suffer the dire consequences of simply being here. Ignorance can be blissful, and it is something that he will have to unlearn, as for now, he is breathing the air of the North, and cannot see clearly enough to think with any reason...

Chapter 5

Devotion

Some people forgive and others wish to be forgiven. It's a repetitive pattern that flourishes from the paints of colourful mistakes and wrong doings that a lot of us are guilty of. I'm no exception. What us humans tend to do is pick out the smallest of flaws from one another, then rip ourselves apart into feuds and battles with no winner apart from Ego. One could say she's always the winner. Our terrible tendencies to always compare ourselves with one another, so that we can only quench the thirsts of satisfaction with juices of superiority and arrogance, could be the only flaw that we ironically are unable to see. We must always be richer than the other one. Always be stronger than another one. Better than so and so. Become more successful than him. Appear happier than her. The comparisons never stop. And if we don't get what we want- we take others down to get it.

They say your actions speak nothing but colours of the dark, but I choose to overlook the shadows, for wherever there is a shadow, there is a source of light. They claim that the flame that once lived inside you, was burnt out, but with a slight blow of oxygen for it to breathe, a fire can reignite itself. I know I would rip my heart out for you, and place it in your needing hand, bleeding with the crimson liquids of hope and friendship, dripping down my fingertips and onto your palm. People always change, but I know there is someone starved of love and support within your strong and brave character. I would let my cup overflow, and let you drink every drop until you were satisfied and let me apologise for the assumptions spat at you by the people who are ignorant of your situation. Within me is a person devoted to people, and I will stop at nothing to help them see that you are not as bad as they make you out to be.

The burning flames of inaccuracies and misunderstandings provide clouds of smoke and mountains of ashes, but why am I the only one suffocating? Is it because you've been in an environment like this for so long, that you've adapted and learned how to breathe in what would be the unbreathable?

They say I do too much for people, but my mind is an untamed mechanism, bursting with affection and compassion, and maybe the red flags they see are just a deep shade of magenta. Only joking. I've purposely worn my rose-tinted glasses, viewing the world through the shades of optimism, hope and warmth. The world is a place corrupted by hatred and separation, so why would we need any more? My heart vows to make you feel accepted, and I know one day your mother will be proud of who you've become. It's been four years, and I've still not given up. Every wound of the battles I've fought, oozes with forgiveness and bleeds with a river of love, and I hope everyone in the world will drink from it.

This is my salutation.

Caught in a feud between logic and emotion, my indecisiveness proved dominant in a situation that was completely out of my control. Bad influences don't exist, there are only people who are tarnished by their past and hardships that leads to their bruised behaviours. I promise I will find you, in the future, if our friendship was supposed to last. I firmly believe that everything happens for a reason, even if the reason is unknown to me, I know in the future the haze and smoke will clear up and I will be able to see how things were for the better. But that doesn't mean I removed you from my thoughts. They always drift back in waves, sometimes tsunamis. You're torn and scraped around each edge of your silhouette, yet you are god's creation and he created you as he willed. Don't let the words of others highlight your flaws, because you helped me for the better, even when they thought it was for the worse.

You speak words of contagious laughter, and I begin to wonder about the times that you may not have been so lively. All I know of you is nothing negative, I believe everyone here today is a work in progress. The majority of humans stumble over rocks or pebbles, and others stumble over boulders. We have no right to judge the marks that appear as wounds on each other, no matter how repulsive they seem; they're just scars to reflect another calamity that we have gotten through. You don't deserve harsh treatment by people who are unknowing of your qualities that redeem you. I'm so glad I met you, and I hope to see you again, but until then, farewell.

Chapter 6

Intangible But Absolute

Intangible but absolute, a new bond created from the essential materials of pure trust, shining laughter and fine companionship. Your light can terrify the dark, so I would confidently walk blindly in any direction and know that I would reach the given destination in a safety. Someone different from those of my past and unique compared to the unmet souls of my future- a figure who squeezed the poison from the numerous gashes tattooed on my previously devastated heart and eased my ailing with nothing but the presence of your constant affability. Only words of goodness could slip off the tip of my tongue to describe the lights that you lit up with the embrace of our friendship. Intangible but absolute- no distance could stretch us apart enough for anything to fall into pieces in our hands, and even if they did, we would sculpt something better from the shards, causing the emergence of another priceless treasure.

Your persona is one intertwined with glistening sheets of aurous, and your smile elucidates any doubt that there are any people of good left in a planet overflowing with hatred. Integrity is the only fluid that spills through your vessels of warmth and feeds your organ of compassion, beating each pure drop around the body that holds your soul laced with morality. The existence of someone such as yourself is living proof that a state of unalloyed magnificence can be attained, and that people of refined character can not only be searched for- but found. Your traits exude into my veins and enter my blood stream, through every word you speak, whether comprehensible to the common ear, or only understood between the two of us.

Appreciation- a stencil etched within the deepest chambers of my heart, as you glue yourself to each day that I live.

While I was lost, you gave me direction and when my world was in black and white, you painted it with bright tones of positivity. Things can fall apart, but I doubt that our brother-bond ever will. Who knew four years ago that we would've held something like this between us?

Intangible but absolute- the two descriptive words that are to describe the gift that I thank God for. The gift that you gave to me the moment I saw you. You placed it in the palms of my hands, and I kept it treasured ever since. The gift of our friendship.

Intangible but absolute.

Chapter 7

447

I was born as a baby on the third of December,
But 447 days after, was the birth of an ember,
Who I didn't meet until 14 years after.
Each day that I scribe is an addition to this chapter.
Four years have passed by; I am still stuck to your side,
I was blinded by temptation while figuring out my salvation,

The only thing that kept me to you was our determination,
My habit of holding on and your single-minded dedication.

Is your birthday on the 21st, 22nd or twenty third?
You know I'm no good with memory,
My mind is constantly disturbed,
By the chattering of chemicals that bounce in my head,
But you didn't shrug them off, you decided to help me instead,
With your knife of an ear, you cut open my wounds

And I explained to you, and you heard me bleed,
responding with support to every one of my needs,
then closed my cuts and encouraged me to succeed,

It has been three years since; I've still got plenty to grow,
Even though I don't say it, I hope that you know,
How your blissful smile tends to glow,
I wish you constant happiness in a river that overflows,
And you know what I'm like; my soul gets cold then it softens,
And I know I don't really say this very often,
But I appreciate your presence, I
know I have a weird way of saying thank you,
But I'm finding inner peace and I really hope that you do,
You simply radiate a beacon of positivity,
And I pray with all my heart that you fulfil your inner dreams,

But you still train your eyes to strive and memorise,
I'm aware of its difficulty and I fully empathise,
Just keep in mind how much your status will rise,
When I count my blessings, your name is what I say,
And I'm fully aware that I can never repay,
For the goodness that you bring,
The doubt you put away,
and nothing is coming between us apart from 81 days,
And my memory may be rusty, but I answered my own question,
I remember it's the day of the twenty second.
And I still find it funny,

How the world revolves around money,
When people should find souls who turn their worlds sunny,
Instead of drinking down an alcoholic honey,
The ones who value company should consider themselves lucky.

Chapter 8

Fountains

A fountain appeared from the black hole of my brain, watering and feeding every corner, crack and crevasse, flourishing with purity and bursting with a bliss of unmatched intensity. It leaked into my body, flowing into my fingertips and reaching to my toes, whizzing in my mind and gathering behind my eyes. The world was brighter. Louder. Clearer. A name was etched into my mind, a temporary permanent tattoo, for my thoughts would continuously leap and bound from one topic to another, and the name would fade then reappear vividly a few minutes later.

A drizzle of warmth radiated in me internally, tickling every atom of my body, caressing every cell and stroking every psychotic neurone that I possessed. Or was I possessed? Is it true affection that I felt? Or was it the glasses of mania that distorted my feelings? Dismissing the latter, because frankly it doesn't even matter, I let the flow of the fountain devour me completely, my body entering a sensation of weightlessness, floating slightly above the clouds. I could stay here for the rest of my life. Untouched by the ground, or was the ground untouched by me? Answers that I will never find to the questions that will never wane. But just like the moon, I glow. I glow against the pitch black of everyone else's feelings. Is everyone inferior, or am I just superior? Grandiosity had already intoxicated me, and I became addicted. A name resonated with me; and though I knew it would not materialise into anything, I didn't want to forget it. Half drunk on my emotions, any feelings of sedation were completely wiped out by the plans laid out by the chemistry in my mind.

Unsure of the intentions of the other, and unusual mix of euphoria and loneliness is where we lay our scene. It only takes a few moments for someone to make their mark on my life, and sure enough that is exactly what they did. But was I asking for too much? It was a rare but frequent occurrence that disappointment would crash into my life just after the excitement of meeting someone new. But I would rather let them be oblivious to the situation than address it. Confusion invited itself to visit once again. When will this cycle ever stop? When will I ever get a break? But seeds of attachment, affection and admiration germinated from within, maybe I could build something of substance, with just a little more time.

Would I see this person again or would they become only a distant memory of the past, that will haunt me and my inner thoughts whenever they got the chance to? Would I see their face in the faces of others? Would my heart leap into my throat every time I think of them? I had no clue of the answers to these questions, but at this point in time, answers are irrelevant. I'm just glad I had a few moments to remember, even if I would never experience them again.

The air was hot and warm with memories that swayed between my fingertips, slowly disappearing as if they had not existed at all. The grace of fondly remembering someone who you've only just met- and someone who you know you'll never meet again, is something that is difficult to describe to those who have yet to experience it- but it purely is an experience that will leave its mark on the hearts of those who cherish what it means to be in love. Even if it was for a few moments.

Chapter 9

Deep Breaths

A breath coated with nothing but lust in its rawest form. A craving for the impure, an untamed criminal toying with the attributes of my mind, an awakening of someone new, yet someone who has been waking up since the beginning of this current state. Pushed into a dimension of my deepest desires and twisted thoughts, Common Sense would have told me to pull myself back out, but who is he? No one of importance anymore. Crawling underneath my skin, a tantalising sensation of sudden impulses tickled and overwhelmed my organs, dragging me deeper into the mountainous landscapes of my ever-changing mind. From the peaks I would fly, until I fall to my feet and crash into the hardened floor of a depression, but for now let me focus on the course of my highs.

I've always been afraid of heights when I'm grounded, but now I'm soaring. My fingertips could be close enough to touch the sparkling sun, but my mind is somewhere further up. Somewhere so far up that even I wouldn't be capable of bringing it down. And I don't want to. It enjoys the taste of freedom and continuous possibilities that accompanies it on it's travels. But damn, Common Sense and Consequences will hate us so much that it is actually laughable. They hold no weight in the government of mania. Before, I was terrified of the mental vigour that I knew would inevitably be hurled at me, and be mine to keep for a few months, for Mania could use this for his own good, or abuse it and become a powerful source of spite and vengeance. But who cares? This gift has been given to us, and we can use it how we see fit. Some say these abilities can twist into some of a toxic nature, but does it matter? When this form of power dominates everything you do, say and behave, and claws away at your heart and beating mind, addiction is always present. It doesn't matter how things play out anymore. We just want more of what is in store, and what is in store is what we want.

Pull me in, drag me through and toss me into the despicable city of euphoria- AshWays. It's a place that I will happily venture into, and happily have. I wish to explore every corner, walk over every inch and trespass over every boundary. Recklessness is a dangerously fun tendency of all who live here. We act without thinking. Do without considering. Execute without pondering. This life is what we have; and we will purposely exploit it and take full advantage of what we have.

Chapter 10

Prices

Our character has either lost his mind or gotten lost in his mind. I have tried with every ounce of my will to breathe some sense into him, but he will stop at nothing to feed his careless nature. He has gone twelve hours with no food, three days with no sleep and two months with no common sense- yet foolishness is rampant in his ecstasy- filled brain. He enters AshWays's plaza- a huge empire of marble flooring, glistening walls of diamond and a place where only the wealthiest of people could afford shopping.

I have no idea who he thinks he is. A teenage boy, who barely survived the grip of the surrounding desert, wearing clothes that were made from more holes than fabric- believed he was worthy enough of exploring the euphoric city, let alone run down a luxurious shopping spree, was valid proof that he had reached a level of delusional that was most difficult to attain. It was almost laughable.

Every step I took was weighted down by the mass of the bags which were held in between my clenched fists, but I was propelled forwards by the presiding excitement and giddiness, which dragged me and pushed me from shop to shop. An exchange of money for goods that I will never use, never want and never need, but the only good these goods were for where to be hidden away until the summer of my life would build a creative idea which would naturally find its way to me, and only then will I find a purpose for everything that I had carelessly bought.

The thrill of purchasing, the satisfaction of transactions and the pink glasses of mania collectively came together to blind me from the money which was slowly diminishing away from my debit card. My pockets were full of emptiness. I was racing, sprinting and scurrying my way through a manic frenzy, the shopping bags vomiting out contents of receipts, receipts and receipts. Do I like this shade of blue? Is this jumper my size? Would my friends like these teddy bears? What do I fancy to eat? Questions that never required an answer. But it was never, do I have other priorities where this money could be spent? Do I even have enough money to buy all these things? Should I spend this money for a temporary explosion of dopamine, or should I save it for a future eruption of serotonin?

But all of a sudden, I become the self-proclaimed expert in resourcefulness. I become a gatherer of materials for plans that are yet to be created. Prices are just labels. Money is just paper. They hold no value apart from the value which we attach to them. Money has no worth, it's what we can buy with money that gives it it's desirability.

Chapter 11

Fevers Of Friendliness

I would attack everyone with kindness if I had to. The world has come to such a state that people are starved of the simple necessities to feel warmth, love and peace. A fistful of gentleness is what everyone needs, and something I will give to the entire population of people who live here. I have so much to give and none to take, my selfless tendencies begin to awake. Awake to such an extent that old hatred slips away and is substituted with a drizzle of affectionate honey which I choose to share with everyone who wants a taste. Sticky and viscous, the convivial honey is the perfect ingredient to sweeten everyone's lives, from those who have been starved of it, to those who have been overfed by the bitterness of abhorrent aversion. Burning with flavourful colours, the Northern Lights of my mind illuminated vividly and offered their generosity to the two corners of my lips.

I was set to share this infectious disease of elation and satisfaction, of comfort and friendliness and of magnanimity and unconditional love, as who knows which lives it could heal? It could change and morph each life that it touches, and the unknown possibilities of how much it could impact those who receive it bubbled up the excitement within me, like a vigorously shaken can of soda, frothing and erupting with immeasurable levels of vehement jubilation. Can you imagine the cheers of the children in this world, the smiles of gratitude from the elderly and the joyous expressions of those we love, if we just reflected behaviours of devotion and selflessness to everyone around us? Optimism is the poison that pumps through my blood. We could do so much for the world, if we only just tried. A self-given mission, to restore world peace suddenly becomes a responsibility of mine.

Chapter 12

West Of AshWays

The Northern segment of AshWays had proven disastrous. Driving myself into a reckless shopping-spree, chasing down a new friendship while losing another and convincing myself that I had the power to restore world peace - these were the behaviours that slowly seeped into my system, and who knows what else I would have done if I stayed there any longer? Would I have become one with everyone else- a person who'd throw myself into hapless optimism, impulsive promiscuity and into an insidious bliss of unknown consequences? The North was pretty for sure- the epitome of a cyberpunk city, lit up by the ecstasy of the people who lived there as well as the blinding neon lights that blossomed and bloomed from every building. But something of it made me feel uneasy. Everyone was too joyous- and too much of a good thing never ends well. Sex was the exotic currency used, and everyone there was wealthy. It was a place lost of morals and felt as though the society of the North was completely disconnected from the rest of AshWays. I did not have the chance to learn the name of the woman who I met, for as soon as she offered me the drink, it fizzed down my throat, the world became a dizzying whirlwind of colour and then darkness. What could have been hours later, I woke up, buzzing with a germinating energy that fed itself more and more, and catapulted me into a mental space of jubilation. The affects wore off a few days later, after I had foolishly followed the emotions that I could not control. It was then that I began to reflect. It was then that I decided to run. Run anywhere- no objective of where was necessary, whether I reached the East, South or West was irrelevant, as long as I crossed the borders out of the North.

After days of trekking past boastful buildings, crowds of temporary trysts and through the humid air, I finally reached the threshold into some place new. My clothes hugged onto my skin, so much so that when I pulled the fabric away from myself and let go, it would return and stick back, as if my sweat were a magnet to it. I looked into the horizon and let my eyes feast on the land in front of me. It was the West.

It was a land, void of laughter, and it was said that within it was a tyrant void of morality. His twisted actions would govern the land and he'd provide for the people by demolishing them one by one. He was a figure to be feared, a force to be reckoned with, and on the Western lands of the euphoric city, grounds dusted with sand, he was a quencher of thirsts, by flooding their minds with ignorant malevolence. His beard was as dry as the ground beneath his feet, and his cracked heels violently addressed the floor, blistering with the sun's merciless heat, with each step. With fistfuls of crumpled paper clenched in his hands everywhere he went, they said, if you were to befriend him, that you'd be taking more than a dozen risks. He held authority, yet barely showed himself, and was always draped in fabrics torn and tattered by time, yet he was always there, driving the residents towards a trap to help them escape his own crimes. His palms were stained with invisible blood, yet they chose to overlook them, for the assistance he provided them, meant that he was beloved. He was ignorant to my presence, but they all said he knew; since he would keep count of the number of footprints left behind each day, claiming there should be one less pair each time the sun would rise. The purpose of the sheets of paper were still unknown to my limited knowledge of this sector, but my intuition spoke to me, saying it had something to do with the burning scent that the air would continuously carry throughout the day.

The Northerners were vivid, loud and bold, oozing with chaotic characters and inattentive actions. Each part of AshWays was full of different and distinct characteristics. With no one in sight, it was impossible to tell what the Westerners would be like. Not a single soul was captured by my fatigued eyes, which constantly scanned for any form of life.

The land was nothing like a city. Skeletons of houses were distributed in a random fashion, and they were sparse. The number of people living here must be few. The air was choppy and hazy, sliding my view in and out of focus, and the skin at the back of my neck began to protest and peel against the scorching heat. The entire landscape was a canvas of lifeless yellow and tired brown. I strode forwards and then I saw him. He was no more than 5 feet tall, and his hooded clothing choice hid everything about him, apart from his sinister smile that revealed his decaying teeth and rotting gums. But his identity was validated by the presence of papers, clenched tightly in his wrinkled fingers.

The residents all crawled out timidly from their houses. They were modest in number, a couple dozen at best. It was hard to imagine that this was everyone who lived on an entire stretch of land, compared to the North, where you couldn't walk two steps without numerous pairs of eyes being aware of your every move.

He began to speak; words booming out his vocal cords, with a voice as rough as sandpaper and as dark as charcoal. He recited a speech about escaping lost promises, every word filling the empty air, and diminishing every remaining sign of silence that existed in the space between us, then looked me in the eye. He told me I was running out of time. Confusion gripped me. With that, he stepped towards the crowd, who had gathered in a semi-circle around him, and licked his lips. A tremble broke through a man who was trying his best to keep his composure, and the tyrant caught him, like a shark sniffing out a drop of blood in the ocean. Dropping his papers, he placed his fingers into the neck of the innocent. Then squeezed. And squeezed. And kept on squeezing and did not let go. Those who were watching were motionless and emotionless, as if this were a common occurrence and they had become numb to anything that would normally shake even the bravest of hearts.

He did not let go until the skin of the man had turned lavender purple beneath his fingers. Then he released him. Holes were seen on the throat of the innocent as his lifeless body smacked the floor, the impact echoing and bouncing off my delicate eardrums. It dawned upon me just how precious but feeble life here can be.

Death was a daily ritual for him- the one who provided for the society by destroying them. The rest of the gatherers waited patiently. Fingers dug deep into his pockets; the tyrant brought a lighter into view, and simultaneously, the residents began rolling up their papers. Disgust punched my stomach and wrapped itself tightly around my organs.

They sliced open the corpse, which was a real, living being a few moments ago, and piled his flesh and bones into their papers. Then a line was formed. A queue to the tyrant. A flame was touched to the end of each paper, one by one. The other end was placed into their lips. Each person would inhale for a few moments, collecting the taste of the deceased in the back of their throats, then exhale and release a toxic gas of blood into the poisonous atmosphere. Smoking a carcass. Smoking the body of someone who was once part of them, and tomorrow, it could be any of them.

The tyrant looked back at me and smirked.

"Join us." he beckoned.
I found I was drawn to him. I found something of his aura, difficult to deny, and so I stepped closer, and soon enough, I had a small, rolled up spliff entering the threshold into my mouth, as the bitter taste of burning bones and human flesh embraced my taste buds and filled my nostrils...

I felt weightless, as if I was floating, and my brain screamed an alarm into my ringing ears as I began losing control of my body. A knot formed in my stomach, tightening itself like a snake squeezing its terrified prey. A sudden beacon of light enveloped my sight, blinding me, and I yelled out in frustration, just as I heard the yells of others burst out from their throats. Then there was darkness. Then there was silence. Silence once again...

Chapter 13

Somebody

Together, we smoked, during a short period where time felt as though it had stopped. Your only contentment stems from the intoxicant that you inhale, one that used to be alive. A feeble heart that once latched firmly onto the concept of friendship, love and forgiveness, was soon to be blown out like the flame on a candle. I melted the wax from your ailing soul, but you thought the heat was too much, and would soon throw sparks of pain at me, an individual who wanted nothing more but the best for you.

The protagonist has found himself in the company of someone else; but company in the West is often unheard of. Betrayal sits patiently behind every rock, tree and bush, so do not expect his intentions of purity to last very long. The Westerners are ruthless killers, aiming for nothing but authority and power over one another. They feast on weakness, and as warned, the longing for positive qualities in another can be a vulnerability; with a cost difficult to pay. He must not trust a soul here, but it appears as though he already has; and its someone who is notoriously known for placing a knife in every back turned on him. The protagonist's fate now has either one of two directions: kill or be killed.... and if he chooses to kill, the formidable force of the West may become his to possess...

Maybe this will be the end for him. Maybe he will give in to the masquerade of friendliness being shown to him, and maybe he won't see it coming - and the person he thought he could trust will once again bury his familiar knife of lies into his next victim.

We can only hope that our protagonist chooses mind over matter, chooses logic over emotion or feels the correct emotions of hatred, indifference and a numbness to everyone else's needs. The West is unique in comparison to the rest. They hold onto grudges like their lives depend on it, because they do.

Chapter 14

Ally

A heart of integrity is what you hold in the auditorium of your ribs. Its function is to pump your blood of wholesomeness through each artery, and that if you were to ever bleed, each drop would be the reforming rain to a seed of dishonesty on the land's-tired surface. Your blood would nurture the seed, until a flower of soundness and goodness would sprout upwards, blooming petals of rectitude. Gratitude is the only thing that I can offer to you, and I know it's not much, but it's all I have. You supply so much succour and solace when the harsh conditions of the West feel as though they would destroy every ounce of willpower left within me. The land here is barren and broken, but you help me see through the dusty storms of sand and debris and opened my eyes to see that there can be good in every bad, and bad in every good. You kept me alive, and for that, I'd never be able to repay.

Until now, my journey into the AshWays was one of isolation. Though, I cannot deny the pure excitement I experienced on my travels, an experience shared is an experience doubled. I hope you're here to stay; a permanent companion with whom I can travel this foreign land of beauty and elation with. There would be no one else who I'd want to ration parts of my life with; you, yourself and the completeness of your qualities is enough. I would stop at nothing to keep this comradeship, if you asked of me to reach to the moon and take a piece of its blissful glow, I would strive with every ounce of strength and determination that I could muster, to fulfil your request. I had only known you for a little while, and you had already left a mark so permanent that it stained through the fleshy muscle of my heart and leaked its ink, dripping relentlessly onto my tired yet hopeful organs. Everyone knows my soul is a delicate one, yet I could trust you to hold it with the softest touch and most tender clutch, without breaking it, whenever I needed someone to rely on.

The strength of our connection is undeniable- it can withstand the strongest of blows of force from the words all those who believe they can strive without a worthy companion, in the in-discriminatory land of the West. They believe that only weak people rely on each other, and their weakness is a vulnerability that will be exploited by the people who they think they can trust the most. But we proved them wrong. We prove that two people can be allies in a land that demands people to survive on their own. Call it magical, call it too good to be true or call it whatever you will- but a connection like this is one that holds so much meaning to me, it's engraved and stamped in perpetuity in my memory, and I passionately believe I can never lose you.

Chapter 15

The Betrayer

Surely the inevitable happened. They both trekked their way further into the West, with foliage and vegetation beginning to become more prevalent across the land that progressively became less barren. Suddenly, an oozing wound spread across our character's back, a knife of steel lies, and manipulation dug itself into his flesh, eating its way deeper into him. He cried out in agony and in pain, but his companion threw his head back and laughed out loud. Red blood coated his companion's fingers, painting their way up to his wrists, and he left his red-handed fingerprints on the base of the knife. Our protagonist longed to set it free but every movement of his was excruciatingly painful. He wished to rip it out eventually.

They say he's a dangerous person, because he doesn't forget. He plans to make nothing more of his betrayer, than a human cigarette, that he will smoke when he is nothing but lonely and alone, and when the West's insidious bliss of isolation breaks in. This betrayal has left him shaken, as pain appears from the tip of each of his neurons sending agony through every synapse, which would diffuse into the next neuron and begin a surge of sorrow through his body, in the form of fading electricity as his entire nervous system collapses. He looks back and the betrayer is gone, leaving him stranded in the midst of a scrubland, half forest and half desert. Our protagonist lays down on the floor, he whimpers and quivers in anguish.

The betrayer should wear a warning that would read "I'm a disgrace and I'm doomed", painted with the most fitting ink-his blood. For our character begins to feed on the characteristics that the West provides him with. He turned his pain into power, and he is set on taking an eye for an eye. The betrayer taunted a tiger, he woke up a beast and he should understand that whatever pain he feels from now, will be the cause of our protagonist's actions.

Mercy is now absent in our protagonist's toxic blood, it's a black liquid poisoned by hate, yet it is the liquid that is vital to his survival. They say the earth shook with every step he began to take, the wound in his back still painfully making its presence known to him, but with a strengthened resolve, he was determined to carry on walking.

The betrayer should keep his eyes wide open- watching for our protagonist to reenter his life, and destroy it slowly but surely, killing him alive, allowing him to suffer the pain while being slaughtered. Who will the betrayer go to when his body is buried by no one but the wind and her debris? No one will remember him, but he will be remembered by the protagonist for the pain he first inflicted.

A plan is etched into our protagonist's mind, and maybe it is a little too far, but that won't make him hesitate. He plans to befriend his villains. He plans on making his betrayer beg for forgiveness, but I will protagonist will murder him and slaughter him one hundred times over, laughing at his helpless corpse.

Our character believes he used to be weak, but now he howls and revels in the resolution that's coming. "Forgive and forget"- the rule book for those who are setting themselves to fail. Our character's dawn of darkness spreads over the horizon of his charcoal heart , as he writes down his own rules- "remember and punish". That is why they say he is dangerous- he doesn't forget.

Chapter 16

Voices

They refuse to quiet down yet silence me completely. They dance around my furious mind, fiery and molten, a lava glowing within it, threatening to erupt.

" We are real"

Are they real? Are they not? Where do I draw the line to differentiate between the realities of the external world and the entities that whisper their shrieks through my mind and into the environments around me. Everything melts together; sounds and colours- all the same shade of confusion and panic. These voices scream in the deafening silence that stab my ears' delicate skin, and I bleed in terror.

" We are here to stay"

They belong to no one, yet there is so many of them, torturing my insides, their sounds whipping my core, sending shudders down my spine and my eyes began to water. What is going on? A disruption to the ironic balance that held my grin intact for so long, these voices race around the marathon of my encephalon, the nails of their volumes hammered deep within, bursting out floods of agony and uncertainty.

" You wanted more, so you are getting more"

Criminals. They morph their sounds together, into an ear-splitting dirge, each word holding a fascinating amount of depth.

My eyes scan my surroundings. I'm alone. But not alone. They accompany me from within, and I'm in no denial of their actuality. They reside within me but play around in reality, claiming the world as their sinister playground. I beg them to quieten down, in fear that....

" We feed off manic blood"

... in fear that others will hear.

They drip off my cerebrum like honey, sick and sweet, and invade every other silent, sprinting thought; their footprints stamped deep within my limbic system.

" We won't..."

" You should try this because maybe it will help..."

" Run"

The voices. They leave their handprints all over the temporal lobe, clutching and gripping it with fists clenched tightly, they speak with such authority, but understanding them is beyond me...

Chapter 17

Intrusive Thoughts

A memory leaks into my mind,
As blood leaks from my thoughts' hands,
Vengeance is what I will buy,
Regret is not part of the price.

You trespass onto my mind,
Venturing deeper- you poor unfortunate soul,
The thorns of my mind will peel your flesh off,
But let that be only the beginning.

These voices speak to me, excited to see a death,
Laughing hysterically at the thought of your dark blood oozing,
From freshly cut wounds,
It was wrong for you to wrong me,
Their speech makes all sense,
I'm nothing but a mirror for you.

My behaviours are built from the cement of your actions,

So, if you resent me, you simply resent yourself,
I did nothing but breathe a lake of comfort into your desert life,
But you polluted it with your words and bit every finger of my hand,
The hand that was prepared to feed you,
Provide you with nothing more than support,
But they do say that cheap people can never afford expensive things,
Believe me, there is nothing cheap about the hatred I deliver to you,
It's rich with the darkest thoughts and most twisted of ideas,
I gain nothing more than pleasure, from seeing you struggle in pain.

Forgiveness is a choice- and I choose to ignore it,
For it's easier to wrap the energy of my mind around a phantom who knows the art of imitation,
You cut me with a needle,
So, I'll skin you alive,
A fair trade,
A transaction that will drown you in debt.

I won't shift the blame onto you,
But none is on me,
You've done nothing but harm the friendliness that I gifted to you,
No insurance can cover the cost of the bruises you painted it with,
Your paintbrush being your tongue,
Your colours being your words,

My battlefield being my weapon,
My weapon being my thoughts,

This is no case of misreading the roles you played,
You claim to play the victim; yet you inflicted the first wound,
You've crossed paths with the right person to wrong,
As i have a feeling no one has put you in the place where you belong.

So let me stop talking, and let me save my breath,
For it will surely be gone with the laughter that will be left,
Left behind as your corpse will soon become devoured in the satisfaction,
The satisfaction of watching you unable to pay the prices of the actions you once did.

I can become the epitome of petty,
The best example of vindictive,
But I will only have these titles if there was a reason to hold these within,
Within the deepest chambers of my heart, where nothing but darkness spreads.

Chapter 18

Satisfaction

There's a hidden premises deep within a tangled foliage of violent vines and sinister thorns, home to a treasured chest of diamonds and jewels. Only the foolish would be tempted enough to attempt to grasp a handful of these goods- so of course I stumbled through the web of clawed vegetation, led by the one who they called my demon. He was mysterious, mean, and his face held a curved smile and eyes of venom green. Blood oozed from my drained face, painting my skin with crimson ink that seeped into my pores and dried to form lines of crusts on the borders of my countenance. The darkness of the beautiful night encompassed my eyesight, as we followed the scent of greed and urgency, the aroma of promised goods wafted up my nostrils, as the silhouette of the building grew closer to our eyes, against the black velvet blanket of the sky.

The sound of breaking glass and the sight of an empty room; we invaded the property, assaulting its windows, twenty meters high, and six feet up into trouble. Protesting ropes stretched against our body weight, threatening to snap without warning, but we crawled in, our pupils taking a few mere seconds to adjust to the new depths of darkness that surrounded us.

A scream of agony and a yell for help, within a heartbeat I learned to trust the enemy instead. The flow of blood was halted from crawling past my wrists and ankles by stinging lines of copper-wire, digging themselves into my skin and gnawing away at my flesh. I was silenced by a plaster of tape, that held my lips together, muffling even the smallest of sounds that my voice could muster. My demon threw his head back and laughed out loud. Body left to lay in the four-walled cage of gloom, my heart dropped, as I watched him abandon me, climbing back out the window that we had both entered from.

There's a hidden premises deep within a tangled foliage of violent vines and sinister thorns, home to a treasured chest of diamonds and jewels, and an internal screaming soul, that struggled to release any sounds to the external world. A shadow emerged from the carcass of the shattered window. A knife was pressed firmly against the wires that held me captive but were then used to contain him instead.

A scream of agony and a yell for help, only this time it wasn't silenced. I let him beg for the mercy that was slowly slipping from my pure heart. But I kept him contained until the sun's soft rays tenderly wounded the West's land, so I could observe his terrified eyes. I threw my head back and laughed out loud, as the edge of the knife was hauled into his delicate skin, slicing open wounds, but keeping his life intact. Shrieks of anguish, brimmed over the edge and spilled into the room, scalding the air trapped in it. Piles of his skin were treasured, placed neatly in the corner of the room, and puddles of blood swamped the floor, as he begged me to let him die.

There's a hidden premises deep within a tangled foliage of violent vines and sinister thorns, home to a treasured chest of diamonds and jewels, and a screaming soul. He questioned my actions, claiming he had good intentions, but they say a saviour's words can be laced with lies. I cackled and let him see my teeth before he was put out of his misery.

I was left with the building to myself and eventually found the dust coated chest, after hours of scampering through the rooms cloaked in black. I drowned my hand in the materials of value: gold, sapphires and diamonds, and proceeded to leave the way I had entered the premises, but just before my hand placed itself on the frame of the window, a pair of venom-green eyes illuminated in the reflection of the shards of broken glass that lay scattered, and carpeted the floor, along with the help of a skinned body and dried pools of innocent blood. Along with the eyes, a curved smile began to grow. I'm glad I met my demon- he proved to me I was weak, as tendencies of him began to grow inside of me.

Chapter 19

No Hard Feelings

Anger and resentment are the last emotions I'm capable of feeling for you, believe me. No, honestly believe me. I have no ill feelings towards you. I just wish you dead. No. I wish you a long life - full of immense suffering. I wish your back aches every night before you sleep, and it puts you in such a state of agony that you can't function the next day. I wish your eyes turn bloodshot red, from the tears that you shed from every calamity that you struggle to overcome. I wish your mind gives you no rest, and that guilt and regret are a constant form of companionship for you. I wish you befriend them, because I wish for you to know them very well. I hope that your siblings turned out to be nothing like you.

I don't wish for you to be healthy, but I want you to be healthy enough to live through all the pain that I want you to endure. But honestly, I have no ill feelings towards you. I only want you to live through each second of the day, hoping you were dead. I hope regret eats you alive, leaving you bleeding and battered, your heart swollen and sore, and I hope your thoughts will trail back to me. I hope every breath you take is heavy with remorse and is weighted down by the mass of despondency. But I hope you do well in life. It is said that the wicked get no rest, but when you do, I hope it's short and fleeting, and I hope that every small thing that goes wrong for you opens another wound in your twisted black heart.

I hope you bleed.

I hope you cry.

I hope that when your mother tells you that she loves you- that it's a lie.

My heart holds no room for hate, but I fucking despise you. But you should believe me when I say I have no feelings towards you. You're someone who makes everyone's day harder. You hurt others, because you can't stand yourself. My heart bleeds for you, I sympathise, and I pity you. I wish you get better from the disease that makes you act the way you do. I hope you recover. I also hope you don't. Because I know if you don't stop acting the way you do, then you won't stop being hurt by the people who used to love you. I wish for you the best of the worst. But no hard feelings.

Chapter 20

Be Careful...

The thunder of my heartbeat vibrated my chest, echoing over every cell of my corrupting body and my mind fixated on an idea of many ideas. Thoughts come and go with ease, but in this case, easy come is not easy go. I latch onto the first thing that my mind captures, disposing of any opinions on how insane it may be. A lot of people have questioned my sanity, in a place where they are not to question it. They are so fascinated by how my mind works, that they do not realise themselves how no one is safe from it and its growing power.

How liberating does it feel to know everyone is wrapped around your fingertips? It's a sensation that I am happily becoming familiar with, but don't take this the wrong way-I still am a man of morals. I will not harm the innocent-only those who threaten to prey on my giving personality. They will surely perish under my soon to be reign of the West, and when I claim it as my own; it will be over for the souls who once did me wrong or are hoping to do me wrong. Watch patiently, as their intentions will shift from attacking, to begging with mercy, but no mercy will be shown, and no mercy will be given. This is a place where everyone has one chance- fuck it up and you will surely have not another chance to redeem yourself for it will be the end of you. Mistakes are what makes us human, yes, but they are not what keep us alive. Intelligence is a virtue that can assist in our survival, so be intelligent and do not carry yourself into my bad books- as it will be something you will forever regret.

Names are carried on a list of stencils, so that even an eraser cannot remove the names of those whom I shall ambush. Human blood has the tendency to spill at even the slightest of cuts, so to them: prepare to be releasing seas of the bodily fluid that has the purpose to aid your survival. You will no longer survive the Ashways, or my wrath.

Chapter 21

Don't Tell Me What To Do

He hated being told what to do,
Despised being controlled,
But the irony of it all lay within the chemistry of his mind,
Which would control him,
His friendships,
His money,
Every aspect of his breathing life.

He refused to believe there was anything to be fixed,
So, the stubbornness inside of him grew like a germinating seed,
Where he repeatedly ignored the advice of those around him,
They should've been warned: don't tell him what to do,
Don't tell him to fix a problem that he can't see,
Don't tell him to listen to words that he can't hear,
He believes he's having a time of ecstasy that can't be taken away,

He was once told that even science says gold cannot rust,
But what if the metal he found appeared to be gold but was something else?

Why would he drink poison if he claimed he was thirsty?
Why would he fulfil his desires with twisted mindsets leading to the most painful of consequences?
Was it that he loved being where he found himself?
Or that he loved being in a place other than the dark?
They say that euphoria can turn you blind with its beckoning beacons,
He deliberately stares right into the light,
Burning away at his retinas and stealing his sight,
He is left as nothing but Mania's puppet,
Being strung along; every decision he makes is not his own,
The irony of it is so clear,
How he claims he listens to no one,
How he claims he hates being controlled,
Yet he is the one listening and being controlled.

Chapter 22

Retaliation

Power can be abused, and when you feel like you hold it between your fingers, you will stop at nothing to use it how you want to. I understood why the West were so reluctant to reveal their sector of the city to anywhere else. The Northerners are too feeble. Too fascinated by human socialisation and emotion to be able to adapt to the Western segments. Here, it is each to their own, and each of us have an objective. Each of us are fed by our villains- we are fed names of the people who have slighted us, wronged us and done nothing but humiliate our morals in the lives we used to live. The West provides us power to reach out to those people and gift them a beautiful retaliation. Here, we are not in need of love, friendships or warmth, instead we flourish on the coldness that snakes its way around our souls, forming our sinister intentions.

We see nothing wrong with our visions. An eye for an eye, after-all, is the national anthem of our hearts. The more power we grasp, the more we can act on our thoughts, and the more we act, the more power we attain. It's a vicious cycle that the victims can do nothing about. Make no mistake, we may act disproportionally, but we do not prey on the innocent.

People tell me I'm evil. i'm malevolent and that I carry no substance of remorse. The latter is true. Why should I feel empathy for those who have hurt me? They have been warned that I can become just as brutal as the tyrant of the West himself, and I know in the future, I will be glad I met him. He was the one who offered me a puff of the 'human cigarette' , and the taste of it gave me a sickening awakening. A side of me that finally could see how kindness could be a weakness, and I watched slowly as those past parts of me; the attributes of the Northerners, fell from my body and became nothing but ash in comparison to the burning fire of fury inside my cold and callous heart. The sight of blood spilling from the bodies of the people who have abused and rebuffed my kind-hearted ways is what fills me up with joy. I don't enjoy making problems- I am a problem, and I thrive in my being.

But curiosity is a fascinating frame of mind- and it always gets the best of me. The West has offered so much to me that I can only begin to imagine what the other sectors of Ashways are willing to give to me. So far, I've been given a taste of ecstasy from the North and a crown of power and control from the West. What if the South and East give me more to add to my list? Is this what AshWays is about? To provide residents with a quality dedicated to each of the sectors, and the sum of four qualities will equal to the promise of euphoria? I was never good at maths, but this seems like a promising formula. My mind was set. i was to set off to the South and steal what would be mine to keep.

Chapter 23

South Of AshWays

My eyes feasted on the river's water that reflected a dozen shades of purple from the irradiation of the city's landscape. This was almost identical to the North, and nothing like the West, but having a flowing river divide itself and run through many of the city's roads, I could tell that there was something different about the South. The air was heavy with warmth- an attribute that bought back nostalgia from the Northern sector of AshWays, and just like the North- the Southern sector was the squeaky-clean model of what it meant to be a dystopian, cyberpunk city. Where the North had lights of multiple neon colours dancing through its air, the South was dominated by the sight of fresh violet, scars of heliotrope purple and leaks of Byzantium lights, all dripping exotically from the tops of buildings, surrounding and illuminating them, like mesmerising halos of colour. They sprouted from the ground and flooded the floor, beaming their glow onto my face, and the face of every passer-by. I had a feeling the residents here were going to be similar in character to the people of the North- driven solely by emotion. A craving of wanting to discover their habits took hold of me, and I started walking, with the soft crunch of pebbles under my feet, announcing my arrival to the residents.

They looked like maniacs. Each person who i glanced at, had dark under-eyes, and you would have expected their characters to be sluggish and lethargic, as indicated by their physical attributes, but they were all buzzing and moving with alarming speeds, like a grist of agitated hornets. Only they were not close to being agitated. Smiles touched their faces; all women, men and children, and they wore the most extravagant outfits. Women were seen draped in gowns of silk, often paired with necklaces made from the purest forms of gold and glistening rubies. Their sleeves were half rolled up, revealing tattoos that snaked their way up to the elbows of each arm; markings of names, and decorations of artistic flowers deeply etched into their fair skin. The men had extraordinarily little to hide about their spending habits too- each was fond of wearing suits of either deep navy or matched with the whiteness of their female counterparts. Most of the men also accessorised their wrists with watches of diamonds and jewels, all shining under the gentle glow of the moon's light, and the illuminated buildings. The air carried the aromatic scent of extreme wealth, endless receipts and lives of luxury as children scuttled around the adults, throwing their arms up in the air and shrieking in excitement as their parents would chatter in groups of pointless gossip.

This was a place run by the energy of each individual soul, each one playing a vital role in up-keeping the explosive nature of the sector. The attributes of the people became evermore clearer to me: expensive, dramatic and hysterical. These people live by the law of emotion, much like the North, and had their hearts open to living together, with everyone's success belonging to everyone. Unlike the West, where everyone was each to their own, each looking to tear one another down in a brutal battle of violence and bitter revenge. The West demanded its inhabitants to become solitary and to never suffer the touch of another human life again, but the South... the South's function was built on the foundation of love, devotion, wealth and emotion. The survival of the biggest hearts.

I still had to find the reason behind their lack of sleep. Their eye bags were the most distinct feature on their faces, though the women had attempted to conceal it with their dramatic show of makeup- sparkly eyebrows and colours so brightly painted on their faces that it was nearly frightening to look at. What was keeping them awake? It was not as if only a couple of people had the darkening circles under their bright eyes... it was everyone. What could possibly be providing them with so much energy, if their physical appearance indicated a severe lack of sleep? It was a mystery that I was itching to uncover and solve.

Most people would have left AshWays after figuring out just how tragic this place can be, but the South was a promising piece of land indeed. I felt as though I finally found the place that was meant for me. The place in AshWays where the legend stemmed: a place of extreme euphoria. This could be it. This could be what I was searching for all along. The struggles through the desert wasteland, the intoxicating nature of the North and the bloodthirsty identity of the West, had all led me here: the South. I needed not look any further- I had decided that if this were the place for me, I would never leave- and I had a feeling deep inside of me, saying that it surely was the place that I could finally call home...

****

He is the most foolish of fools. He can never learn from his mistakes. Why can he not see that there is no place for him in the unforgiving lands of AshWays? Our protagonist will suffer again, but in the South, pain stems from a different source. He will suffer the consequences of past actions, that he will find almost impossible to forgive himself for. He will remember every detail and feel remorse in places that he once thought he'd never feel ever again. His mind will chase him into the shadowy depths of the unknown, ambushing him every second of the day, through the hurtful complications of the tragedy he caused. This time there will be no escape. He had managed to wriggle his way out of the North, before it took its death grip onto him, he managed to run out of the West unharmed, before it could skin him alive, in the same fashion that he skinned his enemies, but this time, the South won't be so forgiving. Pain comes in all forms and colours. Each holding a unique shape and shade that hunts down the vulnerabilities of an individual and attacks them at their moment of weakness. How has he not yet understood that in AshWays, appearances can be deceptive? In fact, they always are. There is no hope for him. This is where it will be the beginning of the end for our character. I shall bid my goodbyes, before I witness him driven insane by the phantoms that rule this place. The irony of this all. His hunt for euphoria will only lead him to his destruction.

****

They say I'm in the place where fairy tales don't come to an end, a place where I am promised to be full of joy and high spirits. I may become addicted, but I've found the place that they said was impossible to find. I had crawled my way through the desert of despondency, lost myself into the North, cast myself astray into the West... all to finally find a mind at peace in the South. No more problems, no more troubles and no more calamities.

****

They say everything has a reason, so there should be a reason why the desert was designed to try keep people out of AshWays. But the ignorant mind will not even begin to trace these comprehensive thoughts, they'd only get dragged into false promises and scarred visions of all the ' greatness' that this city can offer. He will surely regret it. But it is already too late. What he is also oblivious of is the ever-changing landscape outside of the city. To get in- he must cross a desert, dry and torturous. But that is the easy part. When people had previously attempted an escape- the desert was replaced by swallowing waves of a cold and furious ocean. No soul made it out alive. It is the ever-darkening secret of AshWays. It doesn't make sense, does it? How can the same piece of land be a desert yet also be an ocean? It is a matter of perspective. Either that- or just the fact that a lot of things in this city do not seem understandable to the basic human mind. We can only grasp so much with so little knowledge of the places that surround us. He is doomed. Either the city will kill him, or the ocean will. I've seen this pattern before, and our character will become nothing, but another echo of a victim AshWays has claimed.

They think they finally have the secret to happiness in their hands, offered by the city, then they become devoured by the evil entities of the city. Happiness turns to regret, and they try to escape and that is when they drown in a depressing sea of chilly water.

He won't be the first and surely won't be the last...

Chapter 24

Isn't it funny?

Love isn't just a word to describe a romance. It is a feeling. An emotion. A state of heart that describes the connection that you have to another person, whether romantic or platonic.

Isn't it hilarious when the person you love the most is the one that can inflict the most damage? Isn't it funnier though, when you ignore all the red flags and warning signs, out of love for this person that you so surely believe you can 'help' or 'fix', because even though your instincts tell you otherwise, you choose to ignore them? But isn't it even funnier when they hurt you and you give them permission to, and their narcissistic tendencies begin to show, and you don't see red warning signs, you just see an 'off' pink? You make a fool out of yourself- a laughable joke that never gets old.

They claim that you are foolish and weak. But I don't think so. I think there is nothing stronger than being capable of showing love and affection to people who may have been hated for so long in their lives, that they only know to show hate back to the world. People bring to the table what they have been given- and if someone brings you hostility and you still give them all levels of your love and trust, it reflects just how strong of a person you really are. You aren't afraid to be vulnerable. You aren't afraid to show them what they are missing. You aren't afraid to fight your cravings and temptations to react to them how they are acting towards you. You're capable of love. You are capable of love that holds depths deeper than what most people can afford to offer. That's something to remember. You know nothing more than to give your innocent heart and mind and soul to the people who have been left in the dark and need light but do not know it. Isn't it funny how to be strong, you must be vulnerable? Isn't it funny how people will mock you and taunt you and tell you that you are wrong for doing what you believe in, for doing what your body tells you is right and for doing what every atom of morality screams at you to do? Isn't it funny how they will criticise you for doing what they will never be able to do? You are someone who loves to care. You are someone who does not give in to hate. Hate and grudges have no place in your heart. At least for this person that you are thinking of right now, whether it is a lover or a friend. Isn't it beautiful that you have found someone who you would rather be hurt by a million times over by them to lose them? Do you not think this person is a gift to you, if that is the price that you are constantly willing to pay, despite being in debt? In debt with yourself, but you will still give more of yourself to this person. Do you not think that you have an amazing intuition? Do you not see how you will purposely ignore it for the soul that has changed your perspective of people? This person, regardless of how toxic they were to you, clearly is special. Isn't it funny that in a world where hate outweighs love, people advise you to hate the people who you love? But even if they are right, you refused to give in to the dirge that they speak, and you continue to gift your gift affections, adorations and love to the people who give back to you the contents of their twisted hearts. But you and I know that no heart is born twisted. Love is weird. Love is strong, and even if you had to let them go, just remember that kindness is never wrong.

Our protagonist ponders on these thoughts as he reflects on what he has done. Guilt is never an emotion that can be shaken off with ease. Maybe he will learn from it, or maybe he will cherish it. For killing and hurting someone who once meant the world to him offers him guilt, is that not a sign that this person still means the world to him? Is it not a sign that people make mistakes, and that one moment of fleeting anger does not equal to how people view each other? Once people that offered a hand to one another, then turned arch enemies who both had intentions to impose damage to each other, and only one felt the blame and took the guilt like a seller would take money. That is our protagonist. Is it not a sign that even though his actions were laced with abhorrent hate, he now feels dreadful for it, and does that not show that he has a pure heart? People's actions are not directly linked to the state of their heart. It's linked to the state of mind. This is a principle that can be applied to the victim as well as the person who lay the first wound. So, with that in mind, our protagonist silently forgives the one who first hurt him, even if he does not get forgiveness in return.

Chapter 25

Sleepless Nights

My creative juices are full of flavour , spilling their contents onto this plain piece of paper with the natural flow of thoughts that seemingly won't come to a halt anytime soon. They accelerate with every passing second and whiz around my mind like a thunderous hurricane, spinning me into another one of the week's sleepless nights.Invisible fingers hold my eyelids wide open; they stretch my eyes out and numb any sensation of fatigue. Talking to my thoughts, I listen as my mind responds with speech so clear and auditory that I struggle to differentiate whether I've heard or thought something. What is this new level of insanity that I've reached?

It is 3am and I'm sprinting marathons around my castle of a room, while a rush in my chest simultaneously blossoms; an energy that keeps on giving, and I'll keep having conversations with myself, even though no one else can hear me. Dialogue with my bloodshot eyes, whispers with my heightened sense of hearing and gossip with the shadows that morph into silhouettes of people in front of my eyes.

The energy within me sends thrills down my spine; ones that are similar to strings of electricity that keep me alive. my days and nights have all leaked together- there is no separation, while my restless mind still wants to decide what I should do next. Should I call a friend? Draft a poem? Bake a cake? Ideas fling themselves towards me like intangible boomerangs.

It's 5am and I begin texting paragraphs, paragraphs and paragraphs to the people who are still sleeping. It is an internal treason that I've lost all sense of reason, but I welcome it with a manic sense of hysterical glee. I begin to act in ways beyond the common man's comprehension. It is my sixth day without sleep, I forgot to mention. There's a smile on my face but everyone around me is frightened. I can't place a finger on why, since to me, my life has only been brightened.

Chapter 26

The Things I Would Do For You

Look up to your dreams and gaze upon them as they come true. They say I can make the air between us warmer and that I can make the night sky roll out above us, divulging the array of stars that would shine above us. They say everything I touch can turn to gold, and gold is a metal that can resist the urge to rust. Instead of falling, we are levitating in a state of love, and I can make the stars twirl above us, lighting up a display of beauty, but a beauty that cannot compare to yours. I can provoke the energy between us to erupt with a volcanic surge of obsessions, instead of it slowly fizzing out into nothing. I can make many things happen that you are yet to discover. I can make your moon dissolve any darkness that still resides in your mind, banishing the shadows of uncertainty that might be dancing in your conscience . We can meet under the velvet night sky, in a place of secrecy and lust, and you can feel as my touch embraces your precious soul, and I can be that irreplaceable, missing piece of the puzzle of your life, making it complete and fixed.

His soul has found another. Call her a soulmate if you will- and maybe, this time only, the future for him looks bright. The law requires a journey to be one without the distraction of love, but our protagonist's heart has opened up, after closing down in the West. This is a rare occurrence for anyone, since the West is usually a place that would seal the hearts of its inhabitants permanently. From what I can see, she's a person with a heart so pure, it glistens with a polished sheen of absolute integrity and every time he glances at her, his heart leaps and his eyes irradiate a gleam of awe. She is the dawn to his hope, and he is the moon to her night sky, a perfect match made for each other. Besides the friend he had acquainted in the North, she is the only person he has met on his travels that I approve of. There is something unique about this love, a quality that is undeniable. Something that takes them both to places that they've never been to before. Their minds collapse in a puddle of sentimental endearment for one another, and their hearts rise like the birth of another daybreak; a sun arising from its murky horizon. Every word they exchange, flies into the sky, where it will stick to the beam of stars that they stand under, the silver light bouncing off their glowing skin. This woman: she possesses a nature unlike any other. Every breath of hers carries a scent of unflawed excellence, every heartbeat sounds the melodies of unrivalled charm and every time she blinks, her eyes reopen with a blissful grace. Her pupils are pools of honey, shining brown in the fragile moonlight. Her body is a work of art, and her brunette hair is composed of soft strings of the sun; silky, smooth and voluminous. She is one to keep.

Chapter 27

Fires Of A Forest

Do you remember how it felt when we first spoke, both of us ensure of the other's intentions, blanketed by shyness as we would watch a small flame begin to form? Was I seeing what you were seeing? Were you feeling what I was feeling? Did you read my mind when the unspoken' I love you' boomed through the feeble voice that spoke in my conscience. Skip a few months forward into the future, and the flame fed itself, becoming a blossoming fire of passion and undeniable heat. A priceless jewel, in a world of dusty rocks, your individual shine was unique and supplied light to my glistening world. I know I would reach up to the sun if you asked me to, and give you a slice of its golden sheen, if that was what you asked from me.

My spinning thoughts are now dizzy, accompanied by our connection of love and intimacy, which cements us to each other, not a single crack in the bridge of trust that we built. You're an ancient fantasy in a modern land. I would tend to your every need, and you would tend to mine, I would tailor my heart to yours, a design sewed by the thread of time. A picturesque silhouette of absolute beauty, dipped into a river of priceless personality, you are created in such a way that I admire and respect you for every word you say.

We would stand under the radiance of the full moon, just inches away from each other, and my sight would dive into your pupils, pools of golden honey, just to make sure I've got the colours right. Your pulsating heartbeat would be a melody heard with the lullaby of your rhythmic breathing. The air around you would dance and pirouette in a luscious shade of joy and security. You convince me that love is more than just a currency, I need not to dig my fingers into my pockets in exchange for a person of good.

Like fires in a forest, you melt away my heart, and place within it nothing more and nothing less than the delicate sprinkles of adoration.

Chapter 28

Forest Fires

She was a flame that flickered in the darkest of nights,
Igniting hope and warmth,
But hoping they would never collide,
For something so strong can also be feeble,
Every second; the fire became brighter

A beacon that shone effortlessly,
Her light caressing the darkness of my walls,
She burned them down with nothing but elegance,
And left the pungent fragrance,
Of smoke, ashes and wood,

Left behind in a pile of dust,
Are the roots and trees of:
Fear,
Shyness,
And broken trust,
She warmed up my world,
And burned down my walls,
A beacon of admiration,
Uncertainty is still a possibility,

But her heart's warmth speaks for all.

Chapter 29

Drive

The back of the leather seats hugged me, with arms of warmth and comfort, as I stared out the windows, admiring the breath-taking sight of AshWays, the place of promised ecstasy. The car was a pearly white and fitted perfectly in colour with the vibrant neon colours which were seen all over the city. On buildings, on the floor, and even streaks of purple and yellow lights whizzed around in the air, like moving segments of the northern lights. Everything was blindingly vibrant. My pupils burned from the beauty they were taking in from the city around me.

The snarl of the engine echoed menacingly, caressing my ears and vibrating down into my chest, as the car sped down the road. Accelerating more and more by the second, the thrilling sensation of freedom and speed filled me up, and the wind tugged and pulled at my hair as the roof retracted. Strings of hazel silk whipped themselves violently, and I had noticed I had taken my cap off and let the freedom of the wind skip through my strands. The sounds of ecstasy's erupting volcano and the hurricane of impulsiveness colliding with each other created a beautiful melody alongside the harmony of the wind's flute. Neon lights slid passed me every second, so much so that I couldn't even make out any signs or buildings. I was driving dangerously fast, but I loved it. The world became a labyrinth of blinding colours, as I blasted my way down the road, which seemed to elongate itself further and further. I couldn't see the end.

Like a bullet picking up speed in the air, the car was moving with a reckless speed, but I couldn't feel any of it. It was at that moment when I felt myself become weightless. Mania stole my mind. I took my hands off the steering wheel. The joyous and reckless habits of Mania dominated my behaviours.

Chapter 30

Scarred Visions

Rhapsody is a common feeling in the South. It is something as common as the air that would be breathed in and would act as a drug to the people already affected by its hypnotic features. But the South doesn't just provide people with heightened feelings of joy; it heightens all their feelings, those of good, and those of bad. This waters the seed to enable them to sense emotion through the profound of their 'mindscapes.' But this also means that pain and misery will be amplified and experienced with immense torment from memories which will be triggered by these feelings. Memories that will creep up on the protagonist and consume him, tickling his heart and becoming too close for his comfort. They will devour him and scar his vision, being the only thing he can see, and being the only thing, he'll not be able to unsee.

It's a twisted paradox that Ashways is. Maybe the more sinister side of The City Of Euphoria is revealing itself through the mask of the South, and the people who live there. This place, after-all, is supposedly the 'peak' of joy and jubilation, but a rainbow cannot be formed with only just sunlight, and surely the ratios must be proportional. The brighter the sun; the heavier the rain. It only makes logical sense that way.

But as we have established, logic gallops far away from a place that is run by pure emotion. Let us hope that our protagonist stays safe, for I am beginning to worry for him...

Chapter 31

Memories

The chorus played through my mind like a hypnotising piece of music, taking me off my feet and catapulting me into a dizzying dance of unequalled gaiety. The bass of insanity once again took hold of me, and disregarded any sense left over in my conscience, as I let myself become hurled once again into a frantic frenzy of hazardous contentment. Lights of my mind boomed effortlessly, and they sparkled and glistened with such a brightness that it travelled through my retinas and reflected out of my dilated pupils.

I became obsessively dependent on the rush that fizzled and gushed through every cell of my living body, and it held an attribute of familiarity. This was exactly how I felt in the North. Should I leave the South? Yes. Will I? No. The high is much too precious of a mental state, to give up just for protection over a few detrimental aftermaths. Besides, I have experienced this before, and can learn from my past mistakes. I just need to avoid any delusional thinking and avoid letting emotion steal my logic.

My mind flashed back to the memories of the people I had met in the North. The friend I had to let go of, and the new friend I made. I began to wonder where they both were, how they were doing, and did they miss me as much as I missed them? A sheen of pink slowly wrapped itself around my heart, as I fondly reminisced on the nostalgia and comfort that the memories began flooding me with. Everything slowed down while it was also speeding. My vision became scarred and blurred, the canvas of a perfect city night-sky, illuminated by the smiles of people of glamour, and city lights that could render anyone sightless, became a smudge of colour and beacons with an auditory touch of laughter and giddy cacophonies that sprouted from all directions around me. My heart shook and shattered against my ribs as it hammered itself with such force that it bruised my bones, but still, a smile was worn across my elated face.

My eyes were stretched open, and I had forgotten to blink. My pulse rebounded in my ears.

My mind then shifted to the person of the West. Memories of when we met, his soothing approach which eased my anxieties along with his habit to find a solution to every problem. The smile on my face intensified. Then... the knife that broke my skin. The fountain of blood that stained my back. The excruciating pain that germinated and grew inside my body and crushed my heart. My hands turned into clenched fists. Then I remembered how it felt to skin him alive. To rip layer after layer of his skin. To hear him beg for mercy. To listen to the desperate wails, escape his struggling vocal cords. To see his blood, create a mosaic on the tower floor. To open up a chest full of goods and steal it from someone who once planned to share it with me.

Hysterical laughter gripped me, and I had completely lost control of myself. But then- more memories came. The vision of the tears in his eyes, the look of confusion and fear that ripped my soul and the sounds of his last breaths that lingered in my eardrums. The laughter stopped. In its place was a trance of crying. Steady rivulets of tears flooded down my cheeks as I began to question myself. What have I done? Where had all the friendliness of mine disappeared to? Why was I so consumed by vengeance that I had allowed it to destroy all sense of humanity from me? Did he really deserve it?

Chapter 32

Still Remember You

I left you to die in pools of blood, when all you had was the best intentions for me. I didn't see that, but now you're gone, and I wished this vision could stop haunting me. I fed my blade into your skin, left you in the state that I was originally put in, but now remorse eats me within, and I shout my apology even though you can't hear it. Your feelings are as hard as concrete, and it's understandable why. I tore you open, wounded you; and let your liveliness slowly die. Your heart was pure, completely clean, and the air that you walked through would always be touched by a heartfelt sheen. I can change my mind each day; but you've never changed your heart, and never had to.

My ignorance is a deadly weapon, and this time it had stabbed its owner. I'm sorry that you can't hear these words of mine and I'm sorry that I became so blinded by confidence that I hurt those who wanted the best for me. I still cherish onto you like a memory that is tied to my heart, and I fondly revisit the times we had before I ripped you apart. I wish for you peace. I wish for you nothing more than a tranquil mind. I wish for you health. I don't wish for my own forgiveness from you. You're nothing but a figure who oozed the essence of what it meant to be unblemished. Regret feeds me with his hands, offering me morsels, but I take mouthfuls.

Now, I wear a bruise on my heart, a permanent mark that aches with each beat of my dark organ. I fell victim to my own impulsiveness, and you were nothing but an innocent bystander- a poor, unfortunate soul who had to feel every ounce of the power of my sick and twisted mind. Power can be a weakness. But it's too late. It's too late for that realisation to arrive. I'm sorry that my existence causes so much turbulence... and I know that this guilt will never subside.

Chapter 33

East Of AshWays

This is a place where the mist of elation can brighten up the lives of those it touches, to the extent where their sight will be lost, and soon, all they can see is a terrifying darkness that envelopes them. This is a place where people vanish. People disappear. People turn into nothing but the air that surrounds them, or they drown into freezing waters, suffocating and gasping desperately for air, before the salty water fills up their wounded lungs., as they fall to the sand of the seabed and never heard from again. The terrifying part- that's what they want. That's what they crave. That's what they miserably ask for- for they believe death would be better than the seemingly endless pain they encounter.

He soon will wish for death too, since it will be the only escape from the slow torture that he will endure. I did tell you: there is no happy ending here. Only an ending. Just how everything has an ending- including happiness. Including euphoria. AshWays- nothing more than a lie told to the youthful minds who are so desperate to find something more than the monotonous, dull pain that continuously throbs in the background of their lives. They want something more, so they hang on to a fib that does exist, but only in a state that doesn't fit its title. It will lure you in like nectar to a bee, then clasp its hold around you, like a Venus fly trap, holding its victims tightly and crushing their every will to live.

It is truly unfortunate for our character has reached the East. This section of the city is like no other. The residents here want to escape. They've come to the realisation Ashways is nothing compared to how it was described to be, and they are perplexed by how many people have been lured into its trap, how many people have decided to stay within its parameters and behave in the way that mania governs them to act in. So many lives will soon be lost, as does every year in the city. The North, South and West are all designed to kill. How they do it is in their own ways. The North tends to throw its inhabitants into a portal of seemingly endless elation, to the point where they become oblivious to their own actions and their careless measures lead them to painful endings. The West is designed to pit each person against each other, drive each person forward with the intention of gaining revenge by killing one another. The South is made similarly to the North, by thrusting its people into the arms of warmth and luxury, but by enhancing their emotions, it leaves them scarred with memories of things they have done in the past, particularly the things done during their stay in the West, and this drives them insane to the point where they reached the East. This is where our character is now.

Perhaps the east is not a destination but is rather a state of mind. They say there is no escape from the East. They say, that although to enter AshWays you must cross a torturous desert, to exit Ashways, you must cross the ocean of fury and despondency of the east. How is it that it is a desert to those wanting to come into AshWays's beckoning arms but is then the opposite: a swallowing ocean of ice-cold waters, ready to collapse on any ships trying to make their way out, or any drowning souls, who would beg to be put out of their own misery.

Chapter 34

Dancing With Doom

You're locked up like a prisoner in my mind, and regardless of how much I try to wash you away, your presence remains permanent and resistant towards any attempt of banishing you from my brain. From my heart. From my soul. My soul. So why is it that you seem to have more control over what I think and what I do than I have? Is this nothing more than a sinister game that you love to play, you mock me in my misery, you taunt me with my remorse, and you laugh at the tears that escape my eyes, they run down my face due to my careless actions. Careless actions that had the intention of causing you pain, but it seems as though I had only hurt myself in the process. As malevolent as you are, I can't see past the magnificent aura that you owned when we first met. It is my fault that as soon as I see a small bit of good in people, that is all I see regardless of how much pain they put me through, but your aura was glistening with life and joy and tranquillity, all of which spread into my empty heart and spread his smile across my face.

Then came the time that you hurt me. The time that turned my pain into fury, and I was set to throw you into the deepest pits of agony and put justice to my name by playing the game of vengeance - and winning. But now, all of a sudden, my morals are hurting. A deep throb of anguish collapses over my head, and I begin to regret every action I held against you. Your innocent soul, who simply makes mistakes, but doesn't deserve the consequences of the mistakes of others. You're a pure heart, who beats positivity into every face that you come across. You radiate happiness, your face oozes with integrity, your smile: it's a blessing and I'm sorry that it's too late for me to be forgiven by you.

*****

The wounded sky bled shades of fiery orange and red, and clouds, pregnant with profound sorrow, wept uncontrollably, spitting at the Earth, and sounding the familiar melodies of hurling raindrops tenderly stabbing the ground. The sun gave her last farewell, before collapsing out of view, and dragged under the horizon. The city was nothing but a sinister maze of darkness and shadows. Shades of dull grey filled up where golden rays of light once resided. Bellowing in agony, the wind tossed the city's debris haplessly, handfuls of decaying leaves, broken shards of glass and sharp splinters were thrown in all directions, adding to the scene of chaos. An aromatic stench of despondency slowly slithered into the presence of the air, poisoning my nostrils, and strangling my throat, as the metallic taste of emptiness filled my insides. Coughing and spluttering, my mind had once again found the stinging sensation of loss, which seemed to ooze into my veins, thickening my crimson blood, and distributing it to every cell, and every atom, that made up my body. The world could be so colourful, while I was so colourless. The relentless rain had combed my hair to my eyes, so I swept it back, and stood up from the shaking ground. Or was I the one shaking? I could not tell. A manic mind, despondent body, and anxious soul made its way deeper into the East of the city that began to feel unfamiliar to him. This wasn't the first time I've felt like this. But for some perplexing reason, everything about everything felt new. Raw. Frightening. It added salt to the wound. A wound which I expected to close up, but continued to pour out gushing streams of blood, painting mosaics onto my mind with the colours of my toxic emotions.

Chapter 35

Ramifications

The deathly silence is broken by the thunderous crash of an inevitable depression, whose reign may last weeks, months or even years. The weakened body of our protagonist is dragged underwater, where he makes no attempt to save himself...

He had the time in Ashways to taste a lie, now he must taste the prices. The ocean wind blows with a passionate force of ruthlessness and wickedness that dominates everything within its reach, stimulating the growth and awakening of waves that rise up to intimidating heights. Navy with a frothing white coat, they streak along the ocean, drowning everything in their path, including our character who tumbles and stumbles under the surface, holding his breath but questioning whether he should allow himself to drown.

Drowning was always his biggest fear. To suffocate underwater, in the crashing darkness, alone and in the freezing depths of water, only to be most likely forgotten about after a fleeting moment in time- to him it seemed as if there were no worse way to go. But then comes in the consideration- what if you were to die from your own brain? What if it caused so much psychological damage that someone was beaten, chased, and hunted down by the organ that is arguably the most vital for our survival? The betrayal of nature; to be gifted with a disease that is so complex yet so simply devastating to possess. It makes you love deeper, but feel much more pain, when pain arrives. It throws you high up into places of vibrant mania, before pushing you down towards a corruptive depression, where every black hole in your path will suck you up and spit you out in a deeper depth of despair. It thrusts you in a sickly, cyclical cycle, yet an unpredictable maze of troubles, bothersome ramifications, and desperate measures.

It cuts you deep, and your body won't have enough blood to even attempt to heal the wounds. Some days you are levitating amongst the clouds and sun of mania, which eventually scorch your fragile skin, and other days you are falling off a cliff, with nothing to hold onto to, just plummeting through the icy air of depression, while your heart leaps out of your chest and every other organ in your body tells you to die. And you want to.

Surely, to die from this disease is worse than drowning, is it not? Drowning can be over in a matter of minutes. With bipolar disorder, it can be an alternating battle of toxic joy, stability, and merciless agony for an entire lifetime, until your actions will dictate your ending.

Chapter 36

Playgrounds

Behind my tired eyes is a phantom's playground. It's a place where everything rots and crumbles, a place where everything good is destroyed and attacked by the phantom's claws of destruction. It's a place where warmth is absent, but coldness is forever present. It's a place that consumes me.

Fatigue kisses me with her soft red lips, her tongue twirling around mine and her saliva dripping endlessly into my mouth. Her embrace is too strong to resist, and she pulls me in closer while keeping me captive in her lips. I placed my arms around her hips, and she beckons me, vowing that she will stay as long as she possibly can.

Behind my tired eyes is a phantom's playground. It's a place where everything rots and crumbles, a place where everything good is destroyed and attacked by the phantom's claws of destruction. It's a place where warmth is absent, but coldness is forever present. It's a place that consumes me.

An illness of my mind, makes me live in two extremes: one of hysterical elation and another of crippling coldness- a coldness that vibrates in my bones and shakes my mind, and holds my heart that slowly begins to lose its beat

I've grown familiar to greet the phantom in my head. They grow with each passing second, daring me to grasp onto the last line of hope, but threatening that if I do so, they will slaughter me. Behind my tired eyes is a phantom's playground. It's a place where everything rots and crumbles, a place where everything good is destroyed and attacked by the phantom's claws of destruction. It's a place where warmth is absent, but coldness is forever present. It's a place that consumes me.

Chapter 37

Dear Depression

Dear depression,

Why do you exist?

Why must you fill every atom of my being with torture that is invisible to those around me, yet so physical and real to me?

Why must you destroy any flicker of light in my life, like a villain blowing out a dying candle?

Why must you freeze my will to live, like winters breath forming over a flowing river, morphing it into a glacier of sadness? How do you benefit from ruining the lives of others? What could you possibly gain from this? Dear depression, please answer my questions which demand answers. Dear depression, respond to my silent screams that agitate my throat but do not escape my mouth. Dear depression, why are you so loud to me, but quiet to everyone else? They questioned whether you actually have a hold on me. They wonder if my pain is something of reality, something you have bought upon me, or whether it is the cause of my overactive imagination. Dear depression, why do you come uninvited, and swing open the doors of my life only to slam them shut in front of my horrified face? Dear depression, why must you be so sly and creep up on me on my journey for the search of happiness? Dear depression, they said you were banished from the land of Ashways.

Dear depression, where do you plan on taking me? Will you lead me to my dreadful end- the end that you so enthusiastically seek to watch me die from? Dear depression, will you be the cause of my last breath?

From,
The protagonist.

Chapter 38

Regret

I remember our bond, but I forgot how to feel. The day and night will cycle over and over again, with the sun rising and setting, and the moon illuminating then dimming, just how our closeness shone with the fiercest of lights, then dim down into the shadiest of shadows. It was said that time is non-existent here in the AshWays, and I never knew the true meaning of that until now, where each second lingers between my fingers, before disintegrating into the air like the memories you have of us. My purpose: now with stranger to me, my existence- now something I do not wish to have and my beating heart- how I ached for it to stop. I would finally be at peace if my blood stopped in its tracks. My mind would be resistant to any pain that will try and inflict itself onto me if I was simply dead.

I once had too many directions, and now I have none. I struggle to see further than six feet in front of me, where I hope to be buried soon. I struggle to hear past the screams of anguish that explode in my eardrums, begging me to end it all, and to end it quickly. I smell nothing but the familiar aroma of depression entering my system and poisoning any last remaining form of joy from my collapsing veins. I taste nothing but regret and guilt in the back of my throat, the bitterness stinging my tonsils, and sliding over my tongue, while my skin is pricked and prodded with the metallic thorns of unimportance. I hold no value. I never did. I never will. Would it be selfish of me, to simply thrust my pain onto the people who would miss me when I'm gone?

This place is awfully familiar. this is where despondency and depression thrive, though no longer in a desert wasteland. Instead, I'm floating in the waves of pain and suffering, drowning in an ocean that knows how to claim me, just as it claimed the rest of the bodies that lay in the seabed below me.

A day does not go past without the thought of you slicing through my mind and engulfing me into a frightening portal of regret and guilt as my aching soul begins to miss you. The feeling doesn't age- each day is as bad as it was the first time. Bloodshot eyes sting with tears that sometimes streak my cheeks, and other times are reluctant and do not make their way past my eyelashes. Other times, the culpability of what I have done punches my chest and makes it close to impossible to get out of bed. I was so hungry for power, that I forgot that the real power was to be kind and generous and loving towards those who hurt you, as being someone who they need, can leave them being a reflection of the person who they once were.

My heart breaks with sorrow, an unpleasant emotion- but at least it is something that allows me to feel. Something that validates my humanity after my inhumane actions caused you mass torment and soreness. Sorrow was an emotion that motivated me to look for AshWays in the first place. To search for euphoria. To search for happiness. To search for anything that will distract me from the internal war I was in- it was myself against my disease, but I had made a mistake, and for it I am terribly sorry, and I will tell you this over and over again, even when your ears bleed from the soreness of hearing my voice and you'd want my existence to disintegrate into the air, just as our bond of closeness once did.

Mania painted me to be larger than life, but that can't be further from the truth. I'm just a fucked-up individual looking for anything that can solve the puzzle in my mind, and for a second, you helped fix it, but you ran away with the necessary piece to complete it. You stole a bit of me and dashed far away, where you are now out of reach.

You might have scraped me, but I had absolutely wounded you in response. A disproportional source of temporary satisfaction, for a few fleeting moments of contentment and thoughts that I had finally gotten even. But now I question if any of it was worth it at all? Maybe I was the cause for our bond to deteriorate. Maybe if I had not responded in such a way, we could have communicated and work things better together, and move past the slight misfortune that you had caused me. Maybe we could have kept our bond from being tarnished by pride, arrogance, and greed. Greed to feed our hunger of vengeance. Power can be abused. I had abused it. Many people will look at our situation and claim that I was the innocent, so then please answer me, and tell me why do I feel so guilty? It's now the only thing that is known to me.

*****

If I were to die without letting you know how deeply hurt, I am by my own actions of detestation towards you, and how it affected the bond we once had, I would die in a mind full of guilt, shame, and regret. As I've said before, I don't expect to be forgiven by you. The things I've said are understandably amongst those that are most difficult to forgive for a person who maybe bruised me a little but did not deserve to be hurt so much by me. Maybe you will find it in your heart, to forgive, but maybe that is just hopeful thinking on my part. News has come to me that you are not doing well, that you are struggling with an illness that claims the lives of many, and though I know I am the last person you want to hear from, I hope you recover, and I hope you will be in a state of health even better than before this calamity rose up towards you. In the brief time that I knew you, you made my world feel like a sanctuary of safeness that would encompass the expansiveness of my encephalon, and your waterfall of abundant care would leak its way into my soul and gush into every cell of my being, flooding it with the sensations of closeness and trustworthiness.

I am happy for the people who will meet you- a figure of wisdom and peace and I know they too will be just as grateful as I am.

They say the good die young- and so did our bond, so maybe it was even better than we both considered it to be. There is no price to be put on the rapport that we confined in the abyss of our souls, and maybe you let your side go, but my side is still imprisoned under the many layers of affinity that I have for you.

Chapter 39

Drowning

A voltaic surge of sorrow propelled me deeper into the swallowing depths of the seas of sorrow. Spitting and spluttering, I was carried far out, with the stable land no longer in sight. The powerful currents heaved me, until I was thrown underwater, suffocating, and drowning in the baleful bliss of unexplained sadness. Slapped by the hand of depression, and punched by the fists of unexplained guilt, my limbs began flinging in a desperate attempt to disperse of the fiery ball of despondency that burned within me.

The fiery ball that shone in the sky above the water's surface, reached into the sea's fluids with its silver glow and hugged me with its fading light. Suddenly, I was floating. The icy oxygen hit my lungs and fed them what they were starved of. Only my face was above the surface. The rest of me was still underwater. The bitterly cold water. It soaked my skin; its salts swam into my mouth with every passing wave. It appears there is no such thing as a good thing. Not one drop of it. Only a promise of severe pessimism; a parasite which makes itself at home in the minds of those whose lives are torn between two poles.

The moon was blinding, and was reflecting off the surface of the water, creating the illusion of an exotic drink of sapphires. I knew that there was no hope left in store, and the pits of my stomach emptied their contents onto the chilling waves around me. Disorientation befriended me, hugging me with one last embrace of comfort that I could feel before I was to meet my end. AshWays- nothing more than a legend told to those who are ungrateful of what they have and would rather chase down happiness in a search for what they want. Suddenly, the rain began to pour heavily down, drenching me, myself, and I, for isolation was once again something that I would meet, just as how it was in the desert.

Thunder rumbled in the clouds above as darkness seeped through the atmosphere, the clouds hiding the moon, disapproving of its hopeful light that was the only source of vision for me. Then it was just darkness. Darkness, with the occasional flash of furious lightning that would rip through my sight with a light so bright it might as well have gouged my eyes out. My mind was dented and sweating with fluids of dejection as I began dipping my head under the water. There was no point in even trying to stay alive. I'd rather it ends here than anywhere worse.

The world around me became a black liquid, hurling me through currents of great strength and tossing me in all directions as I inhaled the bitter water which surrounded me, and felt as it began to seep into my lungs, replacing the air and deafening my instincts to kick upwards towards the surface...

Chapter 40

Blankets Of Warmth

Let us assume for a moment, for the sake of this piece, that the protagonist is sailing on a ship through the East's oceans..

Why is it that love used to mean a painful game, and now it means nothing more than a tranquil heart and a mind at peace? Though my throat is sore and protests against my speech, I would stop at nothing to shower you with my affections. I used to climb mountains for those who would abandon me at the top, they'd leave me in a frost-bitten agony of isolation and coldness, yet you have come at the perfect time, and I assume it's time for me to jump, and to fall. Maybe I would crash and break at the bottom of the valley that lay far beneath me, or maybe you would catch my heart in your palms and nurture my shallow chest, that echoes with the pulsation of my beating and alive organ. Maybe the ones with the prettiest faces do the most damage, or maybe a beauty like yours can destroy the damage that was once wounding my fragile veins, spilling out blood of loneliness into the surrounding body, and marking it with a malevolent shade of maroon. You're a priceless gem in a cruel and callous world, and I hope to myself, praying, that you won't be one just like the rest. My mind can be a dangerous playground of anxiety and problems, the measuring cup of trauma overflows with every passing second and every breath I take. My mind is ripped apart between two worlds- the city of Ashways, and the desert wasteland, and even with a sorrowful heart that is dry and cracked by the desert's dunes of sand and searing heat, you illuminate a blissful smile, that brings a manic sense of joy back into me. I can be hysterical and unpredictable and sometimes my heart becomes tired of beating, but for you I would stay alive for lifetimes more if I could. Your voice flows with the undeniable softness of silk and your touch radiates with a warmth that hugs and cuddles my soul, as you hold me captive in a trance of protection and comfort. My heart is massive, but not big enough to express how devoted I am to you, and if I ever told you that I love you, I promise those worlds carry nothing but the purest form of truth.

You're nothing more than a blanket of warmth that wraps herself around me on my coldest nights, as waves crash down outside my window, bellowing fearful voices of gathering water and collapsing weights of fluid. The ocean surrounds the ship, threatening to swallow it whole, but my eyes shut with a mix of hopeless despondency and the lullaby of your giving amiability and patience that you so effortlessly provide. The lights in my room flicker with shaking hope that I will survive, or that I want to survive, but reminders of the affectionate soul that accompanies me on this trip make constant appearances in my darkening mind. A voice so tired of screaming for health, so fatigued of crying out for a saviour and so sore with failed attempts of screeching for love, can now finally rest and try to sleep through the storm that began its thundering warning.

Chapter 41

I Won't Live Forever

His mind burns and flickers back to the memories of a person whom he understands as the most loyal figure in his life. Someone who he says was born 447 days after he did. Someone who he met in his youth and hopes he will meet again in a pleasant place, where only those who do good and believe the truth will live forever. A friend who he found in the North.

You have unknowingly been keeping me alive, even when I did not want to. Even when I hoped that my blood would stop flowing, my lungs would stop breathing and that I would stop existing, the mere thought of abandoning someone, someone who's attendance in my life is nothing less but a blessing from God, would ache my body with shaking guilt, and I would grasp on something, for just a little longer, so I could hold on and try wait out the agony for your sake. Indeed, I am just a creation, and the creation has limits, but you have constantly reminded me that even the most beloved human was given calamities and struggles, and that the creator does not give a soul more than what the soul can handle. You have reminded me that with every passing second of patience, I will be rewarded for the struggles I so desperately wish to overcome. Your presence in my life has more meaning than you will ever discover, it holds more depth than you can ever dive into, it holds more value to me than the value other wealthy man's money and it could be argued that its important exceeds my need for oxygen, food, and water.

I hope to embrace you in the future, in a place where you will need not to drink from thirst, but you will drink from pleasure, and I hope with my open heart that you will be given a book in your right hand rather than your left. I hope that with every adversity that you silently hide, and that I'm oblivious of, that you find salvation and patience within it, because those are only the things that you have taught me so well, things that I could not even teach myself, no matter how hard I tried, every attempt would be in vain. You're wonderful in every way possible, in every way that words won't even dare to express, and in every way that you won't understand. To me, that is the biggest downfall of all, as you know that you mean a lot to me, but you will never grasp the concept of how much our friendship weighs on the scales of the things that hold the most importance and priority to me. To my core, I am full of unconditional love for you, and when I die, I hope I die before you, because I will not be able to cope with the grief of burying someone such as yourself; I would rather it be me first.

I know I won't live forever- life is just a fleeting moment in time, but within that abbreviated time, I was fortunate enough to cross paths with you and for that, I am forever grateful. I look at you when I am in need of an example for strength and a determined resolve to carry on when things are difficult. I know that one day, there will be only one of us walking the Earth, while the other will be buried under soil and sand, and that death will separate us for a period of time, but if God wills, we will reunite soon after, in a place where only the successful people will live forever. It is said that all your closest friends will be your neighbours, so prepare to hopefully see my face every day in the time where the days are not limited by number.

I know I won't live forever, and one day my time will come, and I hope that I'm buried before you. I wish you get to outlive me and continue to flourish light in the lives of all the people you will meet. I know I won't live forever, and with every passing second, I will get closer to the time where I will be lowered into the ground- hopefully by the hands that belong to you.

When the day comes that I will die, at least I know I had the chance to call you my best friend, and that was a chance given to me rather than someone else. When I die, maybe my children will be the only part of me left behind on this world, and I would happily let them learn from you- someone so pure and perfect in context of the creation, and I'll be proud of who they'll become; people with giving personalities who supply society with peace and happiness, something that you supplied me with while I was alive.

I know that I won't live forever and that one day I will depart this Earth, and I hope the last face that I see is yours. I hope the last person I think of is you. I hope the last words I hear are yours, because your words do nothing but guide me in beneficial ways for this world as well as the hereafter. I hope you're the one to bury me when the time comes. I hope your life is brimming with merriment and that even though it may overwhelm you, I hope that it is only a fraction of what you will feel on the day that we will all be judged on. Not judged by the worldly matters, but by our belief and the content of our character, and from what I know of you, your character is one that burns brighter than most. It is one that can ignite even the darkest of minds in the darkest of places, and what makes it more special is the minimal effort needed from you to make that happen.

I know neither of us will live forever in this world, which is why I'm determined to make the most of it before I die. I never get to tell you how much I love you and cherish your closeness, so let this be only a drop of an ocean of how high I put you on the list of people who I care about.

Chapter 42

Untouchable

A blissful entering of someone new into my life...

Your fingers wrap themselves around the essence of my headspace and your name provides the dripping ink to every conscious thought that blooms like a vibrant summer from within. Is it love or lust? Where does one draw the line between the two? You have been the very cause to the most spectacular pulsations of my heart; where it explodes rather than beats, whenever you cross the tropical landscape of my mind. Maybe it is too early to think of it as much, or maybe this is a sign of something beautiful that is about to be born, but whatever it is; I don't want it to go.

Your purpose is to provide calmness to my otherwise hectic soul, and you do so with ease; proving that it is in your nature to heal and neutralise the acids of my hopelessness with your voice of velvet that soothes my ears. You draw me in with an appearance that almost seems unreal with how perfect it is. I wish I had much to offer to you; it almost feels like an unfair transaction that you leave me in awe with every slice of time that you are thought about, and maybe I just cause you a little bit of excitement in return. I wish I knew what this meant for us; is it the start of something untouchable? Something seemingly unbreakable? Something so phenomenal that nobody but ourselves will comprehend the layers of emotion that we hold for each other.

It may be the case that I am just looking through hopeful lenses, but sometimes dreams do come true, and I feel like this one might, the more I look into your eyes...

Chapter 43

My Light In The Dark

You make me feel as though my body is marked with a highlighter of gold. You scribe a symphony of contentment with the ink of your words into my body, permanent marks of love etched deep into my skin. You collect the stars of my night sky, and hold them in your palm, bringing me a collective illumination of hope when I need it the most. You can take my breath away and preserve it as a gift, you can slow the pace of my anxiety-ridden thoughts with the soft embrace of your lips and I can dance to the melody of our synchronized heartbeats which time themselves perfectly, the sounds of their thunderous booms lingering in my ears even when the only presence of you is in my own thoughts.

I could offer my entire being to you, and still feel as though it is not enough. You are someone who can medicate me simply by letting me fall into your arms or by speaking your thoughts of me to my listening ears. I don't know how to love someone else, and I don't want to. You're more than enough of what I need. I will give you my bloodied heart, knowing you wouldn't drop it, and you would fill the empty hole in my chest with the sound of your ringing laughter and the sight of your smile that competes with the shine of the stars.

Chapter 44

Don't Go

Don't go. Prove my inner anxieties otherwise. You're a refreshing dawn of coolness in a fire of uncertainties that thankfully begins to burn out, but I already miss you even though you've not moved an inch away from me. Your beating heart is where I claim to live; it's a home to me and my ailing soul. Regardless of where I am, regardless of the state of my mind and regardless of the whispers of my mind that haunt me, as long as I'm placed in the chambers of your heart, I'll be fine. Nobody I've come across compares to your breathtaking appearance- you are truly a masterpiece, and I did the right thing by placing my heart in your palm. Hold it firmly, but don't squeeze it too hard- for this is a heart that has been abused by its past users.

The general rule was that the people with the best looks often had the worst intentions, and knowing this, I've given you my full vulnerability, so please don't make me regret it. I looked for love in the wrong places, I searched for trust in the wrong faces, and I found it in you in its most delicate traces- barely there... but there.

Only time will tell, and my anxiety is telling me that you're already on your way... but don't go. Stay here with me; you've warmed my life up in its darkest moments, and if you were to go, I'd freeze. An unspoken promise speaks in the air between us, so stay with me, and let me give you everything of what is left in me...

Printed in Great Britain
by Amazon

77525105R00088